KINDA DIRTY PARIS CONFESSIONS

By
Marc Sotkin

Cover Design by Darren Roebuck

Kind Of Dirty Paris Confessions, Copyright © 2019 by Marc Sotkin. All rights reserved. Printed in the United States of America. No part of this book may be used or reproduced in any manner whatsoever without written permission except in the case of brief quotations embodied in critical articles and reviews.

ISBN 978-164440775-2

*For my parents, Bruce and Ruth Sotkin
who made laughter an integral part of our life,
and
my children for continuing the family tradition.*

ONE

Mickey Daniels was selling his heart out. He had no choice. There was too much was riding on the sale. It took every ounce of effort to ignore that he was in Rosenbloom's Dry Goods, a dark, cramped storefront on New York's lower Eastside. Packed from the dirty, warped wood floor to the peeling, plaster ceiling with an unappealing hodgepodge of low-end clothing and housewares, this truly was the bottom of the fashion ladder.

Abe Rosenbloom's daughter, Celia, a stoop-shouldered, big-toothed girl, nearly six foot three in her stocking feet, stood uncomfortably modeling a loud, flower print housecoat over her street clothes just as Mickey had instructed.

"I swear she looks like Marilyn Monroe in that thing," Mickey pronounced with all the conviction the twenty-seven year old salesman could muster. "Gorgeous. Don't you think?" Mickey added in an attempt to engage Abe Rosenbloom in the sale.

The middle-aged shopkeeper, as worn down as the store that bore his name, was more interested in the elderly black woman picking through the dresses strewn on the markdown table.

"If you like any of those I can do better," Rosenbloom called out as the woman held up a bright blue taffeta gown that would be perfect if she were attending some third world coronation.

Unwilling to idly wait for the return of Rosenbloom's attention, Mickey addressed Celia. "I bet that makes you feel gorgeous," he said, referring to the fuchsia housecoat dotted with bright red roses.

"I don't know," Celia answered shyly. She wasn't used to getting compliments from a young man as handsome as Mickey Daniels. Just about six inches shorter than Celia, Mickey kept himself at a trim one hundred fifty pounds. He was a perfect forty regular. He could buy right off the rack and look like a million bucks.

"Oh, I think you do," Mickey replied with a wink that resulted in a big toothy grin from Celia. Mickey took another flowery housecoat from his sample bag.

"Look at this label, Mister Rosenbloom. You see that?"

Rosenbloom lowered the reading glasses perched atop his head. "It says Paris."

"Yes, it does," Mickey said confidently.

"This shmata was made in Paris?"

"That's a picture of the Eiffel Tower, isn't it? So what do you want to do?" Mickey sensed it was time to move in for the kill.

"To tell you the truth, Mickey, I'm still overloaded from the last time you were here. I don't need anything."

Mickey wasn't about to fold. He couldn't. Sales are the lifeblood of any business and his business was bleeding to death. He went on the attack. "You don't need anything? What are you talking about? You gotta keep up with the fashions. You're in the fashion business."

"Yeah, that's me. I'm Oleg Cassini." Abe Rosenbloom wasn't up for a fight. He never was. It was why his store was a monument to clutter. "Okay, look, give me half a dozen. Make an assortment."

"Six? All right. Forget it," Mickey said with enough indignation to cover his fear of losing the sale. Then, turning to Celia, he ordered, "Take it off."

"Your father never complained when I ordered six," Rosenbloom protested.

"I'm not selling these to any one else on the block. I'm giving you an exclusive. An exclusive, Mister Rosenbloom, and you want six?"

"All right. All right," Rosenbloom sighed in defeat. "Make it a dozen. Do you believe this kid?"

"There you go." Then, deciding that her cooperation earned her an act of extraordinary kindness, Mickey looked deep into Celia's eyes and growled a lustful, "Wow."

She was still wearing a horsy grin when Mickey, his bag of samples repacked, left the store.

Heading down Mott Street, Mickey checked his watch as he passed a storefront with a huge "John Kennedy For President" poster hanging in the window. He had time for one more call before his lunch date. He stopped for a moment and studied the picture of the handsome Senator from Massachusetts. Mickey was considering voting for the Catholic. His only reservation was that if his uncle Heshie was right, laws would be passed requiring everyone to eat fish on Fridays. Mickey walked past two more stores then turned into Abramson's Dry Goods. The place made Rosenbloom's look like a couturier.

Jack Abramson sat behind the cash register reading *The Forwards*, New York's daily, ironically titled, Jewish newspaper.

"Hey, Mister Abramson," Mickey called out as the tinkling bell above the door announced his entrance. "Wait till you see what I've got for you from Paris. An exclusive!"

∽

Nino Lombardo hurled the slightly built Greek truck driver across the narrow alley in the midst of New York's garment district. Only five feet seven inches tall himself, but weighting two hundred and thirty pounds, it would be a mistake to think of Nino as fat. He was a bull.

Nino straightened the sleeves of his black mohair suit after slamming the ex-Athenian into a row of trashcans. The mid-town din allowed the beating to continue unnoticed by the throngs passing by the seam of concrete separating two adjacent Manhattan monoliths. The Greek barely managed to roll away, avoiding one of Nino's savage kicks. Instead of the man's ribcage, Nino's foot hit a trashcan sending leaves of rotting Chinese cabbage flying.

Just as Nino grabbed the stunned truck driver by the shirt and dragged him to his feet, someone finally stopped at the head of the alley to see what was going on. Mickey Daniels watched as Nino drove his fist into the truck driver's mid-section. With the man doubled over, gasping for air, Mickey approached.

"Are we on for lunch or not?" Mickey asked Nino as the brooding hulk contemplated the next chapter of the brutal beating.

"I gotta finish with this guy first," Nino answered.

"How long? I'm hungry."

"Until he pays up."

Mickey watched Nino slap the man twice more before walking over to him. Mickey knelt down next to the man who was now crumpled on the ground, crying.

"Listen, I want to help you. Why don't you give this young fellow the money and I'll get him out of here," Mickey advised.

"What money? I don't know this guy. I don't know what he wants," the truck driver sniveled.

Turning to Nino, Mickey asked, "Did you tell him what you want?"

"He took a loan. I'm collecting," Nino explained.

"Did you tell him that?" Mickey asked in a patient, parental tone.

"I don't know," Nino mumbled.

"Well, you've got to tell him that," Mickey said.

"Why else would I be beating him up?" Nino asked, defending himself.

"I thought he was robbing me," the Greek whimpered while getting to his feet.

"Look, you owe the money," Mickey said, suddenly the peacemaker. "Why don't you pay him something?"

Ignoring the pain growing in his entire body, the truck driver quickly pulled a few bills from his pocket. Nino grabbed the cash and began counting.

"That's everything I've got," the truck driver explained.

"You better have the rest on Monday," Nino snarled.

The man stood frozen with fear as Mickey and Nino walked from the alley and turned down Twenty-seventh Street.

"Sclafani's?" Nino asked, suggesting a lunch spot.

"Sounds good."

They made their way through the bustling garment district. All around them, loyal Teamsters unloaded huge bolts of fabrics from trucks. Racks of finished goods covered with plastic were wheeled down the middle of the street by brown skin men recently arrived from San Juan.

"Hey Nino, *que passo?*" a man pushing a handcart called out.

"Hey, Tito. How's that Rolex?" Nino replied.

"Works beautiful. You got any more? My boss wants one."

"I'll see what I can do," Nino said while examining his knuckles that were beginning to ache. "Can you believe that little Greek prick? Look how I'm swelling up." Nino said to Mickey as they continued down the street.

"We've been over this, Nino. Before you start beating them, you gotta tell them."

"I know. I know. Sometimes I think it should be you working for my old man instead of me."

TWO

A brilliant sun and clear sky made the Bronx Zoo sparkle on a perfect day. Three-year old Matthew McGuire intently watched a male chimp jerk off while the boy's mother, unaware of the graphic scene that would stay with the lad for the rest of his life, kept an eye on the strange woman who had been following them for the past fifteen minutes. The woman, twenty-six year old Tippy Daniels, looked like she had just rolled out of bed. Disheveled hair, no make-up, she wore an overcoat that was much too warm for the day. The hem of a flannel nightgown was visible below the coat. On her feet were fuzzy bedroom slippers. Tippy studied the mother and child and pondered the questions that haunted her incessantly, day after day, hour after hour, for the last year and a half; what was so great about having a kid, why was she devoid of any maternal instincts, how long would this bout of insanity last?

She hadn't always been shrouded in this unrelenting mental fog. She had grown up as Tippy Vanhouten, happy enough in W.A.S.P. Haven, Connecticut, the second child of a sometimes-sober country club mother and an ultra-successful manufacturer/businessman father. Vanhoutens had been making fasteners since Revolutionary days. Nails, screws, cotter pins, you name it, if it fastened one thing to another, the Vanhoutens made it. It was Tippy's father Howell, however, who led the company through the post-war building boom of the late 1940's and 1950's and made the company a global success. Tippy loved watching her father work. Even as a little girl she would sit at the kitchen table watching her father make one of his famous Do It/Don't Do It lists. Howell went through the same ritual no matter what decision he made. He'd divide a piece of paper in half, write "Do It," on one side of the page and "Don't Do It," on the other. Then he'd appropriately list all the pros and cons. Sometimes it would drive Tippy crazy. "Daddy, you're deciding whether or not to make a new size wing nut. Why not just do it?"

"Because, Tippy, that would be impulsive. And you should never do anything on impulse." Then, wondering if he wanted to make a 7/8" reverse thread wing nut out of impulse, he added that sentiment to the "Don't Do It" column. Still, Tippy could see how the business world excited her father. It made her want to be part of it. It was assumed that Tippy's brother Toddy would take over the business some day even though Toddy showed no interest in doing so. Toddy wanted to be a drunk like his Mom. As for Tippy's desire to go into the business, that had nothing to do with Mr. and Mrs. Vanhouten's plan for their daughter.

Private school, cotillions, an intimate knowledge of which fork goes where, young Tippy Vanhouten would be groomed for the perfect life. Her uneventful education would be completed at Daddy's alma mater with her marriage to "the right boy" planned for the summer after graduation so that any meaningful employment would, most assuredly, be deemed unnecessary. This wasn't the plan just for Tippy. It was the blue print for the lives of all her well-healed female friends; college, followed by marriage to the appropriate Presbyterian prince, followed by procreation to insure that the line of barely blue blood would be carried on. In college Tippy majored in Literature so that she could be properly conversant at dinner parties. She also managed to slip in as many business courses as she could under the guise of electives. Her parents' plan was going full throttle until five years earlier when it hit a snag.

It was 1955, when as a college senior, Tippy and some of her more adventurous friends made their way to Greenwich Village to take advantage of New York's liberal drinking laws and to see some real live beatniks. Also looking for bohemian thrills on that very night was young Mickey Daniels. He and his City College of New York buddies were on the prowl for "artistic girls" who, rumor had it, would put out. Instead, sitting at a table in a smoke filled coffee house, Mickey found the very clean, very preppy, Tippy Vanhouten. The raven-haired beauty with doe-like eyes immediately smote him. And so he approached, ignoring the other three girls at the table and focusing intently on Tippy.

From a very early age, Mickey knew he could sell. He was a natural. "Ice to the Eskimos," his father would proudly proclaim each time Mickey convinced his parents to grant his every wish. Tippy's aloof façade was no match for the silver-tongued devil.

"I know you must hear this all the time, but you are the most beautiful woman I've ever seen."

"Nobody hears that 'all the time'."

"Would you like to?"

He had her right then. It was an easy sale because Mickey actually believed it. She agreed to go on a date. That date was followed by another, and another, until they were seeing each other every weekend. Either Mickey would take the train to visit Tippy at school or she'd come to the city.

For Tippy it was somewhat confusing, but wonderfully so. Mickey Daniels was so *not* the man with whom she'd envisioned falling in love. But that's what happened. He was such a character unlike any in her storybook life that she couldn't resist. Chemistry trumped common sense making them both completely, totally, and happily enrapt in love. So once she had graduated from college and he had gone to work for his father, Tippy accepted Mickey's marriage proposal.

For all her parents cared, she might as well have met a reefer smoking, beret wearing, bongo playing, poet that first night. They couldn't see how marrying a Jew from Brooklyn was any better. When the time came, they forbade the marriage, assuming that Tippy's fear of disinheritance would far outweigh her love for Mickey, or, as her father insisted on calling him, that son-of-a-bitch Yid from Brooklyn. They were wrong and refused to attend the civil ceremony performed in a judge's chambers, attended by only his parents and a small group of friends.

Mickey and Tippy settled happily in to a small apartment on Eighty-fifth Street, right off of First Avenue. But it wasn't long after the wedding that Tippy began to feel lost. Mickey went to work everyday. But she... what was she supposed to do? There were no answers in the apartment.

Nor were there any when she'd meet with friends for lunch. "Have a baby," was all they could come up with. The trips to the zoo were intended to find answers. Instead, Tippy Daniels floundered further and further into a dark world of despair.

Tippy waved at taxi after taxi as they sped by the entrance to the zoo. It took a few minutes before Tippy understood why they wouldn't stop for her. She looked like a crazy lady. Why shouldn't she? She felt like a crazy lady. Finally, she stepped directly on to Southern Boulevard forcing a cab to either stop, or run her over.

The driver looked at her suspiciously via the rear view mirror hoping he wouldn't have a long drive talking to someone who wasn't all there.

"Sixty-third in Manhattan, between Lexington and Park, please," Tippy said as she sunk into the back seat. The driver need not have worried. Tippy would spend the ride quietly staring out the window.

Three

In 1960, Sclafani's was simply the best Italian restaurant in a city known for great Italian restaurants. From the starched white tablecloths, to the waiters in white serving coats, to the captains in tuxedo jackets, the place reeked of service. And the food? Grown men regularly burst into tears of joy when first they tasted Mario Sclafani's *Malfalda Domenico*.

Joey Sclafani, Mario's thirty-five year old son, stood at the Maitre D's lectern trying to find a table for the Brooklyn Borough President who had decided to drop in without a reservation. Even though it was only lunchtime, Joey looked like a movie star in his tuxedo.

"They're setting up the table right now. It'll only be another minute, Mr. President," Joey said with great deference. He took extra care not to ogle the politician's voluptuous companion, a woman half the man's age who, if things went well, would play with the old man's *bichcallique* in return for the best meal of her life.

Joey picked up two menus and was about to lead the old ward boss and his babe to their table when he spotted Nino and Mickey coming through the door. Joey walked right by the politician and greeted Nino like a long lost brother.

"Nino! *Como va?*"

Handshakes were accompanied by kisses on both cheeks for Nino. A warm handshake for Mickey followed, as Joey made sure everyone felt welcome.

"Can you squeeze us in?" Nino asked, simply as a courtesy.

"Come on. I got something right now," Joey said while leading Nino and Mickey to the table that, moments ago, had been promised to the local pol. Pulling out a chair for Nino, Joey cooed, "You boys have whatever you want. Lunch is on me."

"That's okay, Joey. I'll pay," Nino protested.

"Don't even think about it," Joey insisted as he snatched two perfectly folded napkins from the table and in one most elegant motion deposited them on the boys' laps.

"Joey I should pay."

"Bup, bup, bup," Joey interrupted. *"Manga."*

"Gratsi," Nino said.

"And be sure to tell your Papa I said hello." Joey gave a small bow before heading back to the lectern where he wouldn't even bother explaining to the Borough President what had happened. You don't get to be Brooklyn Borough President without knowing what's what.

As soon as Joey was out of earshot, Nino said, "I hate when he does that."

"You want to trade?" Mickey said. "You want to take my briefcase and go sell housecoats to the Abe Rosenblooms of the world and I'll have Joey Sclafani treat *me* like a king?"

"You don't know what my life is like now," Nino said with a touch of indignance.

Mickey wouldn't listen. "Hey, I'm busting my balls selling crap that I hate. My wife is becoming like a goddamn zombie. I'm sleeping with a woman who…Jesus, I don't know what I'm doing there. And I don't know if I can keep the business going. And you're bitching because Joey Sclafani practically blows you every time you order a meatball?"

Nino heard nothing after Mickey's confession of infidelity. "You're sleeping with a woman? And I don't know about it?"

Mickey and Nino had been best friends since the day the Daniels moved next to the Lombardos when both boys were three-years old. Forget "best friends," they were more like brothers. They were inseparable. They knew each other's darkest secrets. How was it possible that Nino would not know that Mickey was having an affair?

"Yeah. I'm sleeping with a woman. It's nothing," Mickey said nonchalantly. He reached for a slice of bread and began to butter it, avoiding Nino's stare. But Nino Lombardo's stare was not something a person could avoid. It was menacing, penetrating, and unrelenting. Even Mickey could not defend against it. It only took a few seconds before Mickey cracked. "Put your eyes back in your head, would you. It's Charlotte, at the office. Okay?"

Nino shook his head and chuckled, "Charlotte? She's like ninety."

"She's thirty-two."

"Thirty-two. Ninety. Come on."

"I know. I can't stop. I want to stop. I can't," Mickey said with a real sense of frustration.

"You can't stop? Charlotte?" Nino asked while picturing the object of Mickey's affection.

Charlotte McKinney knew she would never win a beauty contest. Hers was a plain Irish face. She was short, only five-foot-three, and a bit on the plump side. Charlotte did however, in Mickey's estimation, have a glorious set of breasts. Her ass, although it was already headed in the wrong direction size-wise, was still admirable. And, with her teased red hair and lavishly applied make-up, Mickey found her sexy in a very trashy, New York kind of way.

Mickey leaned in to explain his dilemma. "See, she wears...she wears this dirty underwear. You know, not bad dirty underwear. Good dirty underwear."

His interest piqued, Nino called out to Joey Sclafani, "We're gonna need a bottle of wine. Red. Something nice." Nino turned back to Mickey who began his tale of woe.

"I don't know. It just happened. It was the day after my father's funeral. I was sitting at his desk in that shit-hole of an office, and I'm remembering how he used to say to me all the time, 'Mickey, some day this will all be yours.' He had no idea of how much that would always scare the crap out me. And now it was mine. And what was I going to do? And Charlotte comes in to tell me how sorry she is about my father. Well she bends over so we're eye to eye. But I'm not looking at her eyes because I can see down her blouse and that she's wearing this black lace bra. And right in the middle, where the two cups meet, there's this small silver snake head with these like glowing green eyes."

"Getdafuck," Nino whispered in disbelief.

"I'm telling you. She's asking if there's anything she can do but I can't answer because these snake eyes have me like hypnotized. So she catches me looking and all she does is smile and unbuttons another button. Then, she looks out, you know that big window that looks over the factory floor, she makes sure nobody's looking, takes my head in her hands and pulls me right to her chest."

"Get-da-fuck," Nino said with increased interest.

"I don't know, maybe I'm in shock over my old man. Maybe it's the snake. But the next thing I know I'm on my feet kissing her, and I'm grabbing her ass, and she's grabbing my ass, and neither of us is letting go, and we kind of hop over to the window and drop the blinds, and then we did it. Right there on my father's desk."

A captain arrived with the wine. Nino organized his thoughts while waiting for the captain to finish pouring. He took a taste, nodded his approval and waited for the captain to walk away before continuing. "Okay. She had a sexy bra. You were in mourning. You made a mistake. But you can't do this to Tippy," Nino said.

"I know. I love Tippy," Mickey said with all sincerity. "I feel like shit."

"Then you just gotta do what you just gotta do. Break it off."

"That's what I wanted to do," Mickey explained. "So I went to her place to tell her. You know, in case she made a scene or something. I didn't want that in the office."

"Makes sense," Nino confirmed.

"So I go to her place, and she opens the door, and all she's wearing is this black see-through peignoir."

"That's it?" Nino asked in disbelief.

"Okay, underneath there's just a couple of red feathers covering the important stuff. But then she tells me to come in and she walks to the couch, and I see that the back of her undies are cut out so you can see her ass. The undies, they're called, 'dream come trues.' She goes to the couch, opens the peignoir, opens her arms, and I'm a dead man."

"How do you say 'No' to that?" Nina asked, commiserating with his friend. "Jesus. Dream come trues?"

"Yeah. All the stuff she wears has names. Her panties are Fig Leaf Frolics, or Shanghai Show Me's. And on top, it's Mutiny On The Bountiful. She flies this stuff in from the Orient. I'm telling you, its nuts. The last time I went to break it off she was wearing this Uncle Sam hat and she opens her raincoat like she flashing me and she's naked except there's like sparklers going off…I can't stop seeing her, Nino. I'm weak. I'm addicted."

Nino sat quietly, feeling ill equipped to provide advice in an area that he himself had very limited experience.

"I gotta do something to change my life, Nino," Mickey said, his voice cracking as he fought back tears. "My whole life is fucked up."

Joey Sclafani suddenly appeared at the table to ask, "How's that wine? That's from my special cellar."

"It's nice, Joey. Thanks," Nino said without looking up.

Joey, realizing that Nino was not in the mood for conversation, kowtowed away while babbling, "Whatever you want, Nino. Whatever you want."

Nino leaned in toward Mickey. "See what I'm talking about? Why's this guy kissing my ass?"

"What did you think it was going to be, working for your old man?" Mickey asked.

The boys were in fifth grade when it was first spoken out loud what Nino's father did for a living. Vincent Caruso blurted it out during a playground fight. "Your father's a gangster," Caruso grunted while holding Nino in a headlock. Mickey immediately jumped on Vincent Caruso's back knocking him off Nino. After some residual pushing and shoving, like most schoolyard fights, the combatants went their separate ways. On their way home, Nino confided to Mickey that he thought his father was indeed a gangster of some sort. He wasn't sure exactly what the job entailed but judging from the secretive nature of his father and his co-workers, Nino was fairly certain that gangstering was the family business.

The news didn't faze Mickey. After all, what did it change? He wasn't going to stop being Nino's best friend. He still liked Mr. Lombardo who was often home when the boys got back from school and would take them over to Kings Highway for ice cream cones. So Nino's father was a gangster. So what?

By high school, both boys worked for their fathers during summer vacation. Mickey worked in the shipping department of T&T fashions making deliveries and doing odd jobs. Nino did odd jobs for his father as well. Picking up numbers money, dropping off a hot watch, his work really wasn't that different from Mickey's.

Both attended C.C.N.Y. for a couple of years before dropping out. Academics were never the strong suit for either young man. Nino went right into the family business. Mickey got a job as the assistant to an assistant buyer at Gimbel's department store. But after his father's first heart attack, he had to help out at T&T full time. Mickey took an occasional night course at the Fashion Institute of Technology, to learn more about fabric and design. But since sales are what keeps a business afloat, sales is what Mickey was stuck with. For Nino, it was thuggery.

"I know what you're saying, Mick, but I'm not my old man. So why's Joey kissing my ass? I'm me. I'm at the bottom. I beat guys up. I take shit off trucks. I'm just a scumbag."

"Today you're a scumbag. But eventually..." Mickey wanted to bolster Nino's self esteem. "And he has you doing other stuff besides beating people up."

"Still, I don't know if I'm cut out for this. Now Pop wants me to get rid of these designs he bought from some French fuck."

"What kind of designs?"

Nino took a sip of wine and debated if he wanted Mickey to know the details of the job. Some secrecy was always necessary to protect Mickey as well as himself. Finally he asked, "You ever hear of some designer called Armand?"

"The guy's like the hottest thing. Jackie Kennedy buys his shit," Mickey said.

"How do you know these things?"

"I'm in the fucking fashion business," Mickey said, defensively.

"Okay, so this guy stole the designs for Armand's summer line and wants Pop to move them. Now I gotta find someone who wants to knock him off."

"Very funny. Go ahead, bust my balls," Mickey said, shaking his head in disgust.

"What? How am I busting your balls?" Nino asked in all innocence.

"This is perfect for me."

"No," Nino said emphatically.

"You want to sell them. Let me buy them."

"Okay. That's it. Just forget it," Nino hollered. He then stood up from the table and headed for the door.

Joey Sclafani made a beeline for Nino. "Nino, what's wrong? Was everything okay? No dessert? Espresso? Let me brush you off."

As soon as Joey began to smooth Nino's jacket, Nino pushed Joey to the ground. He moved to the door, turning around just long enough to yell to Mickey, "How many times have I've told you? You and I will never do business. Never!"

Four

Tippy sat on the examining table as Dr. James Collins, the high priced Manhattan neurologist her mother insisted she see, gave her the once over. He checked her glands before shinning a light in her eyes and up her nose. Dr. Collins was tall and still vibrant for a man well into his sixties. He had a great shock of white hair that, along with the lab coat and stethoscope around his neck, gave him an aura of unquestionable authority. Tippy, however, was less impressed since during her first visit she had fixated on the slight whistling noise he made when breathing through his nose. He was looking in her ears and whistling away when he proclaimed, "Everything looks good, Tippy."

Tippy gave a huge sigh. "Then why do I still feel this way? Why do I feel so dull? I mean, look at me. I don't even want to get dressed in the morning."

Collins couldn't help but notice that Tippy was wearing a nightgown and bedroom slippers when he first entered the examination room. He had noted it on her chart along with a reminder to speak with her mother about Tippy possibly seeking some psychiatric care.

"You feel that way because you're still adjusting to the Librium," Collins said in the firm tone that made most patients accept his diagnosis as gospel.

"I think it's making me more depressed instead of less. Maybe I should stop taking it," Tippy wondered aloud.

"I don't know about that," Collins said with a chuckle, making her suggestion sound absurd. He was not used to having to cajole patients into taking his learned advice. He was not used to many of the changes he saw happening all around. In Collins' mind a suitable level of decorum was necessary for society to function properly. Walking around in a bathrobe and fuzzy slippers didn't even register on his decorum meter. "You still have those same feelings about not having children and wanting to work, don't you?"

"I guess. I mean I look at mothers and children all the time...and I don't get it. I'd rather get a job."

"And you think that's normal for a twenty-six year old married woman?"

"I don't know." The drug-induced cobweb that encompassed her mind had Tippy confused.

"It's not normal. It just isn't. Believe me, we're seeing this more and more and not exactly sure why. It's so prevalent I've had to come up with a name for it, Rebellious Housewife Syndrome. So many of you young women are too agitated. You want this. You want that. Be a mom, Tippy. The best thing you can do is stay on the Librium. It will lessen your anxiety until, eventually, hopefully, your maternal instincts kick in. It's what's supposed to happen."

Collins could tell from her look that she still wasn't convinced so he brought out the heavy guns. Facing her, he put both of his hands on her shoulders, looked her directly in the eye, and said, "Tippy, I'm a doctor. I think I know a little better than you how a woman is supposed to feel."

He mistook her silence for agreement, walked over to the counter and began to write a prescription. "I'm actually going to up the dosage a bit. It will speed things along." He handed her the prescription and added, "I'd like to see you in a month."

Tippy shuffled out of Dr. Collins' toney brownstone and luckily slid into the back seat of a curbside taxicab just as another passenger was getting out. "Columbia Medical Center, please."

Tippy's next appointment with Dr. Margaret Reed couldn't have been any more different than her office visit with Dr. Collins. The procedures weren't that different; checking the glands, looking at eyes, ears, nose, and throat. It was Dr. Reed who was different. She was young and didn't have the attitude of superiority that doctors so often foist upon their patients. And she was a woman. Tippy hadn't been to a woman doctor before she met Dr. Reed. Tippy spent more of their time together asking how Reed got into medical school and what it was like going to work every day rather than about the clinical trial.

"So, Tippy, have you noticed anything unusual; any spotting, severe cramping?" Reed ran through her standard series of questions although she was fairly certain she already knew the answers. "The Pill," as it was known since its inception, had been approved in 1957 but only for severe menstrual disorders, not for contraception even though it was proven effective. As a result, large numbers of women reported having severe menstrual disorders. Dr. Reed was part of a final clinical study before the Food and Drug Administration would make The Pill widely available. In many ways the trial was mere formality, the final FDA hoops the drug manufacturer was jumping through before certain approval. This wasn't the real medical research Margaret Reed hoped to conduct. The trial was a moneymaker for the hospital and would provide funding for other research projects she cared about. The trial was in its final weeks. The last thing the hospital, the drug manufacturer, or the women waiting for easy availability of reliable contraception wanted was some red flag popping up to delay the final approval.

"And how are you feeling today, Tippy?" Reed had also made note of how disheveled Tippy looked when she came into the examining room. In Reed's estimation, the trial participant was exhibiting symptoms of depression.

"I don't know. Okay, I guess," was the best Tippy could muster.

"And are you sure you're not on any other medication?" Reed had asked the question on each of Tippy's visit. Now she wondered if Tippy's odd behavior was a side effect of The Pill.

"No, nothing." Tippy was ashamed of her present state, ashamed of her lack of maternal instincts, ashamed of her lack of purpose.

"You're sure?" Reed asked before noting her observations on Tippy's chart. If this behavior was the result of The Pill, a correlation would have to be explored.

"I guess I have been taking some Librium." The confession took less energy than maintaining the lie.

"I see," Reed said flatly, not wanting to sound too relieved. "What was it prescribed for and how much are you taking?"

"I've been agitated," Tippy said, parroting Dr. Collin's misguided diagnosis. "My neurologist thinks it will help."

It was obvious to her that, for whatever reason Tippy was taking Librium, it wasn't making her life better. Still, it was not Margaret Reed's place to question another doctor's opinion. Tippy was not her patient. She was a participant in a drug study. Reed went back to her list of trial questions. "And would you say that this month you and your husband had the usual amount of sex?"

Tippy had to think about that one. Had they had any sex? She rarely had the energy or the desire any more. But surely they must have had some sex. "Maybe a little less," she answered.

"But would you say that you and your husband are both still satisfied."

"Satisfied?" The way Tippy asked made both women laugh.

"With The Pill? You're both still satisfied with the birth control pill and would use it if it were available?" Dr. Reed asked.

"I would," Tippy said.

"And what about your husband?"

"He doesn't know," Tippy reported.

This news took Dr. Reed aback. "Oh. I just assumed you would have told him that you've been testing birth control pills. Don't you think he should know?"

"I thought the whole purpose of The Pill was to give a woman a choice so she has control of her own body," Tippy said defensively.

"That's the plan," the doctor said.

Tippy thought for a moment, and then she confirmed, "Well, I'm controlling it."

Five

It was always loud inside the Times Square Playland as a cacophony of arcade noise filled the air. Pinball flippers flipped, sending stainless steel balls careening into bell ringing bumpers. Mechanical quick-draw cowboys fired loud six-shooters and growled, "You got me partner," each time a young player successfully committed make-believe murder. Rows of racecar simulators blasted out the sound of screaming engines and squealing brakes. Still, the noise was not loud enough to drown out Mickey Daniel's renewed assault on Nino as the two of them played on adjacent Skee-ball machines.

"You know I've always wanted to really be in the fashion business. This would do it," Mickey said as he rolled one of the big wooden balls into the forty-point hole. "I don't know why you're being so unreasonable about this."

"You think this is unreasonable?" Nino rolled a forty-point ball of his own before turning to Mickey. "Do you know why guys like me usually hang around with other guys like me instead of guys like you?"

Mickey stopped playing long enough to ask, "Why's that?"

"Because eventually guys like you are going to want to do business with guys like me. And if something goes wrong with the deal you think that because we're friends I shouldn't take care of things. But that's not how it works. If you screw up, I'm just gonna have to do what I'm just gonna have to do. Then I'm gonna have to be unreasonable."

"Nothing's gonna get screwed up," Mickey said.

"That's what everybody thinks," Nino said before tearing his string of award tickets from the machine and heading for the prize counter.

Mickey was right behind. "Look, there's this guy. He was an assistant buyer at Gimbel's when I was there. Now he's at Bergdorf-Goodman. He's always said he can get me in to show my line to his boss."

"So do it," Nino said without looking back.

"I can't," Mickey said.

"How come?"

Mickey grabbed Nino's arm and spun him around. "Because I make crap. And Bergdorf-Goodman doesn't carry crap."

Nino wasn't used to anyone grabbing him. He instinctively pulled away. "So stop making crap. You design something."

"It doesn't just happen like that. Listen, this is perfect. I take your designs and make some samples. I show them to Bergdorf's. If they don't buy, I return the designs to you. No harm done. You sell them to whatever shmuck you want. But if they do buy, I take the order to the bank. They lend me money on orders all the time. I pay you right away. There is no risk."

Nino had to admit that Mickey's plan seemed plausible. He thought for a moment looking for a hole. "Pop thinks these are worth twenty grand. That's a lot of money, Mick."

"From Bergdorf's to the bank. No risk."

Nino turned to the attendant at the prize counter.

"Let me have that big teddy bear," Nino said pointing to a huge stuffed panda seated in a chair.

"How many tickets do you have?" the man asked without removing the cigarette that dangled from his lips.

"Three hundred and forty," Nino said proudly.

"You can get a plastic comb or six of these rubber spiders," the attendant said, pointing to a box of the cheapest novelties that, for some reason were locked away in a jewelry display.

"How many tickets for the panda?" Nino asked.

"Forty-five thousand."

"I'd have to spend like ten thousand dollars to win the bear." Nino then turned to Mickey. "This guy's got a better racket than me."

Mickey was not amused. He leaned in to lend an air of privacy and said, "Nino, it's not my line that's crap. My entire life is crap. If things don't change...I gotta change it. Will you help me or not?"

Nino thought for a moment before turning to the prize attendant. "Give me the comb."

SIX

Nino checked his watch for the umpteenth time as he wolfed down a slice of pizza. Even though the timepiece was supposedly crafted by old-world artisans, who knew where stolen merchandise really came from? Plus this was his first battery-powered watch. The new technology had only come on the market three years earlier. Nino didn't trust the damn thing. No one could tell him when the battery would die, just that it eventually would. It became impossible for him to let more than five minutes go by without looking to see if the second hand was still moving.

He stuffed the last few bites of crust into his mouth and headed down Twelfth Street. He didn't want to be late for his last appointment of the day. It was almost 7PM and the street was practically empty. The daytime throngs had already made their exodus to outlying boroughs or suburbia and the nighttime Greenwich Village scene hadn't begun. Nino liked the quiet streets.

Normally, Nino would feel out of place in Greenwich Village wearing the fashionable but formal suit that was his work-a-day uniform. The Village was where the Beat Scene was born. The local hipsters were leery of men in suits. But as he climbed the steps to The New School of Social Research, Nino blended in perfectly with the arriving students.

The New School, a progressive institution of higher learning, offered upper level degrees – masters and doctorates – in the social sciences. The Continuing Adult Education program provided people who had undergraduate degrees in their chosen fields an opportunity to further their education in a convenient yet challenging part-time environment. Most came to class directly from their day jobs, the women in dresses, the men in suits and ties. Nino did not stand out as he climbed the stairs to the third floor lecture hall. He took a seat in the first row and waited for the arrival of the professor, Peter Ivanofsky, PhD.

Ivanofsky had managed to escape soviet Russia in the early 1950's. A burly man with a ready smile and engaging laugh, the soviet system was just too stifling for the jovial psychologist. Attracted to the academic freedom of The New School, his seminal work on addictive behavior allowed him to immediately become an important member of the school's psychology department. In addition to his downtown night school duties at The New School, Ivanofsky also taught morning classes uptown at Columbia and spent afternoons midtown seeing patients in his private practice. The Herculean workload had him always rushing from one end of Manhattan to the other. Always in a hurry. Always running late. His colleagues would often suggest that he slow down. Perhaps three jobs were too much for one man. What they didn't know was that Ivanofsky kept up this hectic pace, not because of his deep desire to share his vast knowledge of addictive behavior, but because of the massive debts he'd run up betting on the unpredictable horses running at Belmont and Aqueduct race tracks. Those debts eventually forced him to borrow money from one Vito Lombardo who sent his son Nino to collect.

Ivanofsky was now ten minutes late for the start of class. A group of fifteen students had already taken their seats. It would be impossible for Nino to confront the Russian until after the end of his lecture. He would then explain that the first of many high interest leaden payments had come due.

The classroom door flew open and Ivanofsky stormed in. The rushing from classroom to office to classroom always left him ill-kempt, uncombed hair, a shirt tail out, large sweat stains revealed as soon as he removed his suit jacket. Looks aside, his peers considered Ivanofsky a giant of academia.

Before he even got settled class began.

"Nietzsche said that each and every one of us has the power to create a life story where we are the hero. We can make the choice to overcome those little voices in our heads that say we are limited. We have a choice whether or not to live a meaningless life. That means we have the capacity to create happiness. Agree or disagree?" Then pointing to a woman in the second row he asked, "You?"

"I'm not sure that's true. If it were, why would anybody choose to suffer?"

"Excellent question. If all we have to do is create a wonderful life for ourselves, why don't we all just do that?" Ivanofsky pointed to Nino, "You. New guy."

The question caught Nino by surprise and not just because he wasn't expecting to participate. He was surprised that he had paid enough attention to what had been said to have an answer. This was not his normal classroom behavior.

"Maybe, yes. Maybe, no," Nino said. "I mean sometimes you just gotta do what you just gotta do. And you know, sometimes you gotta do things that may not be that nice. How are you supposed to be happy doing that?"

"Sometimes you just got to do what you just got to do," Ivanofsky said, echoing Nino's words. "This man is completely correct."

Nino smiled. His faced reddened. He liked the compliment. He liked this guy. It would not make beating him to a pulp any easier.

"I spent a year being re-educated before I left Russia. The guards, I mean the teachers, at this re-education camp were all so unhappy. They never smiled. They never engaged us. They were as miserable as we were."

Ivanofsky sat on the corner of his desk and spoke more softly. The change in tone grabbed the attention of everyone in the lecture hall.

"But there was this one guard. He always smiled. He always talked to us like we were people, not prisoners. He still would throw us into solitary confinement. He would still take our food away from us if we talked in the mess hall. He just did what he just had to do," the professor said with a nod to Nino. "But he chose happiness in spite of it. Here lies the psychology of happiness, my friends. Here is the secret," Ivanofsky said while tapping his head with his forefinger. "We all have the power."

Nino remained seated until the other students filed out. The two-hour class had flown by. Instead of falling asleep in class as he did throughout high school and during his brief college career he felt energized as he approached Ivanofsky.

"Do you know why I'm here, Professor?" Nino asked.

"I am guessing you are here for some money," Ivanofsky said while gathering his belongings. "I recognize this unhappy look of someone who's just got to do what he just has to do."

"It's no big deal. So where's the two fifty you owe?"

"This I do not have today," Ivanofsky said while smiling.

Normally Ivanofsky's behavior would instantly send Nino into a state of rage followed by some rather ugly strong-arm tactic. Rule number one of loan sharking is that the borrower needs to understand the importance of paying his debts on time. In Nino's experience, the best way to illustrate that would be to begin with verbal intimidation, but quickly escalate to the application of some physical pain. It saved a lot of time if you got to the physical pain sooner rather than later. But, to Nino's surprise, the required rage wasn't there. Ivanofsky wasn't cooperating. He wasn't quaking in anticipation of a beating that he must surely expect. He was choosing to be happy. His attitude threw Nino off his game.

Unable to conjure up the monster that possessed him whenever Nino prepared to deliver a beating, he simply asked, "So what are we going to do about that?"

"I know you have probably heard something like this before," Ivanofsky began. "But I promise that I can pay you next week after class." He truly believed his promise having already placed a large bet on a sure thing gelding running in tomorrow's fifth race at Belmont. Those winnings would surely make him enough to repay all his gambling debts.

Rule number two of loan sharking is to never forget rule number one. Nino knew that. He thought about smacking Ivanofsky around. He thought about returning to class again.

"All right. I'll come back next week. But you better have the money. Don't let me down. I want you to make me happy."

"That I can not do, my friend. No matter what happens, your happiness is up to you. Now come. We go get a drink." Ivanofsky put his arm around Nino's shoulder and lead him out of the classroom. Nino wasn't sure why, but he followed, willingly.

SEVEN

Tippy had a plan; prepare what she thought was Mickey's favorite meal, and then pop the question.

Mickey sat at the dinette table reading the sports page of *The Daily Mirror* as Tippy slowly opened the can of Chef Boyardee beef ravioli. Each turn of the can opener seemed to require a moment's pause to form a new thought. Still dressed in the same housecoat she wore day after day it also appeared as if Tippy had neglected to bathe that day. Tippy gave a sigh of relief once she managed to fish the top of the can off without cutting herself and deposited it safely in the trash. Then, slowly, she turned the can upside down and held it over a saucepan waiting for the tightly packed doughy patties and thin red sauce to ooze out. This was not the girl that Mickey had married and she knew it. She wished she hadn't taken a Librium before Mickey got home. She had to break through the chemical miasma surrounding her thought process.

"How was work today?" she managed to ask.

"Crazy. It's always crazy." Mickey said without looking up.

"Maybe you need some help."

He wasn't really listening. Whatever she had said barely registered. Still, he guessed that some non-committal response was necessary.

"Uh huh."

"Maybe I could help out."

"Uh huh."

"Really? Do you mean it?" All the pharmaceutical mind dulling power in the world couldn't hide her excitement. Tippy momentarily came to life. It was enough to get Mickey's attention.

"Mean what? What?" he asked, now looking up.

"That I can help out at the factory."

"Why the hell would you want to do that?"

"I want to work, Mickey. I want a job."

"Believe me, you don't. It's hard enough dragging my ass down there every day."

"I could make it easier for you. So things wouldn't be so crazy."

"What are you going to do to make it easier for me?" He made sure his tone was dismissive enough to end the conversation. It did not.

"I don't know. You could have me do some of the things you don't like doing. The things that make it so you have to work late so much."

Mickey's face reddened slightly at the mention of his working hours. Too often of late, he wasn't really spending the extra time at the office. He was in bed with Charlotte. Working late, going for long walks, these were the excuses that provided the windows of opportunity for his illicit affair. For a brief moment he considered Tippy's proposal. He wondered if having Tippy at the office would make it unbearably uncomfortable for Charlotte. She might quit ending not only the working relationship but the sexual as well. Mickey longed for a life with a sense of normalcy, a life where he wouldn't feel like such a louse.

"Well?"

Her question broke his train of thought. He looked at his disheveled wife still holding the can of ravioli over the pot.

"I don't think so, Tip. Not now. You could never handle the stress."

"But I want to."

"The answer is, no." Mickey went back to reading the paper.

The ravioli plopped into the pan. Tippy stared at it blankly.

EIGHT

Nino was early for his first collection of the day. Craig Langstrom, the man he hoped he wouldn't have to rough up, worked across the street from a Chock Full 'O Nuts restaurant. Nino ate his date-nut bread sandwich and "heavenly" coffee breakfast while reading *Addiction: Mechanisms For Recovery*, written by Doctor Peter Ivanofsky. Normally, Nino rarely read at all. If he did, he favored some piece of pulpy escapism that featured a scantily dressed dead girl on the paperback cover.

The addiction tome had been a parting gift from Ivanofsky after the previous week's night of drinking together. The next day Nino began reading. And although his progress was excruciatingly slow, he found the subject matter fascinating. This was not easy reading. The book's target audience was graduate students and psychology professionals. In addition, because it was translated from its original Russian, the language was somewhat stilted.

For addicted person denial of truth is function of brain chemistry not conscious effort. Brain becomes most comfortable in this state even if addicted person rationally accepts they have no control over compulsions. Living lie feels better than dealing with truth. Only repeated effort to change brain's chemical response will alter addictive behavior.

Nino thought about Ivanofsky's theory. "*Living lie feels better than dealing with truth.*" Most of the people Nino dealt with were lying to themselves. They had convinced themselves that one more bet on a horse would change their lives, or one more drink was all they needed and then they'd stop. They were sure that just one loan from Nino's father would end their problems. They couldn't see that the transaction would not end their addictive behavior. In fact, the added stress of paying exorbitant interest on a loan that was almost impossible to pay off would only make their lives more miserable.

Nino wondered; how could brain chemistry be changed? Even the beatings he doled out would only temporarily change someone's behavior. He'd beat someone up, fear of another beating would get them to pay him some money, but their addictive behavior, the root of their problems, would never change.

The lusciousness of the cream cheese on the date-nut bread was enough to distract Nino. He looked at his wristwatch. To his relief, the second hand was still moving. It was time to go to work. Getting the money was his job, not changing someone's brain chemistry. Besides, if he helped every Tom, Dick, and Craig Langstrom change their brain chemistry he'd be out of the loan sharking business. For a split second he wondered what that would be like. Fuck it. Time to go to work.

Langstrom was headed to his office at Lehman Brothers when he felt Nino's tap on the shoulder. He immediately went into his song-and-dance excuse of why he didn't have the entire four hundred dollar payment that was due.

Not wanting to make a scene on the busy street, Nino suggested they continue their transaction in a nearby alley. Langstrom had another idea.

"Let me ask you something, do you know any thing what so ever about buying stock on margin?"

Nino hated everything about Langstrom's Eastern prep school tone. Nino felt that every word from Langstrom came through his nose and was laden with condescending attitude.

"I'm not sure you'll understand, Nino, but it's like buying on credit. The brokerage house lets you buy the stock but you don't have to put up all the money right away. Hopefully the stock goes up and you sell it before you even have to pay for it. Does that make any sense to you at all?"

"Sounds like a great racket," Nino said.

"Well yes. I guess in some ways it is. If the stock goes up. On the other hand, if it goes down or if the brokerage thinks you're over extended, they can call in your margin. You have to pay what you owe. Do you understand, Nino? That's why I had to borrow the money from your father."

"What's that got to do with me?"

"Now here's where I'd like you to pay close attention. Not all the stocks in my portfolio went down. I still maintain a large position in quite a number of good companies. Instead of me paying you each week I want to give you a substantial number of shares of Polaroid."

"The camera people?"

"Very good, Nino. Yes, the camera people. I was fortunate enough to get some perhaps inside information from a gentleman friend who works there. In a year or so Polaroid is going to introduce instant color photography. My friend assures me the company is going to control the entire industry for the next hundred years. This stock is going to perform extraordinarily well."

"Well I'm assuring you that I'm about to smash your head into this wall. What's the point?"

"If you take the stock, it pays a quarterly dividend that will cover the payments I'm making to you. And you'll still own the stock. When it goes up, you sell. You're going to make, pardon my French, a fucking fortune."

"So you're not going to be giving me money every week?"

"Have you been listening? You get it quarterly. But it's the same amount. Maybe more. And then there's the aforementioned fortune."

"I don't know. I gotta think about this one."

"Please, Nino. This constant threat is wearisome. I believe we'd both prefer if it came to a reasonable conclusion."

"This stock thing you're doing is just like playing the horses. You need to change your brain chemistry. Otherwise it'll never come to any conclusion."

"Change my brain chemistry? What in heaven's name does that even mean?"

Nino wished he knew. He genuinely wanted to give some sage advice. He sensed that helping Langstrom out of his predicament would be more satisfying than continuing what was truly, by definition, a vicious cycle.

"It means you better have more money by the end of the week." It was a frustrating conclusion to Nino's first transaction of the day. Two more collections and it would be time to meet Mickey for their weekly lunch.

∼

Charlotte McKinney was so accustomed to raising her voice to be heard over the constant sewing machine din that filled T&T Fashions, she no longer spoke in a normal tone. The added volume often made her sound angry even when it wasn't the case. So although she thought she was sweet talking Harvey Miner, an investigator from the Federal Trade Commission, by saying, "I know I promised you he'd be here. But I just don't know where Mister Daniels is," it sounded more like she was annoyed by his presence.

Miner's beat was the garment industry and he was no stranger to the runaround. "I'll wait," he said flatly.

"I can have him call you as soon as he gets in," Charlotte suggested. She was fairly certain the FTC was not there to give Mickey a commendation for being New York's "Above Board Businessman Of The Year." Charlotte had worked at T&T for thirteen years having started right out of secretarial school. She had seen Mickey, and his father before him, cut whatever corners were necessary to survive in the nickel and dime world of low-end ready-to-wear. Miner wasn't the first government bureaucrat with whom she'd ever dealt and he probably wouldn't be the last. She was prepared to stare him down. It wouldn't be easy.

Harvey Miner was a student of human behavior. Over the years he had learned to recognize the slightest change in a person's facial expression that might indicate they were lying. The instant Charlotte's eyes shifted toward the door, Miner spun around in time to see Mickey, who, in returning from an early morning sales call, had recognized the situation and was doing a quick about face.

"We need to talk Mister Daniels," Miner called out.

Mickey kept walking.

"Fine. I'll just close you down."

That was enough to stop Mickey in his tracks. Mickey took a moment to gather his wits then turned and walked back onto the factory floor.

"What's up Harvey?" T&T had been in trouble with the FTC enough times over the years that Mickey felt they should be on a first name basis.

"You know ignoring a cease and desist order is not a good idea. What's the matter, last month's fine wasn't big enough?" Miner said with a slight smirk.

"I stopped using the 'Made In Paris' labels," Mickey protested.

"Really? I just took these out of some of your goods at Kreski's." Miner took a handful of labels from his coat pocket and held them out as evidence.

Mickey took one and held it up to Miner's face. "They don't say made in Paris."

"They say 'Paris' with a Picture of the Eiffel Tower."

"So?" Mickey said defiantly. "That's where the Eiffel Tower is. This isn't false advertising. It's truth in advertising. My father used these for years. What's the problem all of a sudden?"

"You have a week to recall all the goods that have these," Miner said as he returned the labels to his pocket.

"Recall? You're making me take stuff back? Look, maybe we can work something out. Why don't you take a couple of housecoats for your wife? Take as many as you want - the good ones with 'Italy' and the picture of the leaning tower on the label – and I promise I'll stop doing this."

"You've got a week. I'll see you then," Miner said. He walked to the door, stopping long enough to grab two housecoats off a rack, and threw them over his shoulder as he left.

"My god, Mickey, what are you going to do?" Charlotte asked.

"I'm getting out of the rag business, Charlotte. That's what I'm going to do."

∼

Nino ignored Mickey as he perused the menu. None of the Hungarian delicacies tempted him. He didn't really like Hungarian cuisine but Bela Harshani, the owner/chef of Pillango, paid enough protection money to Nino's father that a bi-weekly appearance at the eatery was a requirement.

"Do you know who I met for breakfast?" Mickey asked.

"Willie Mays." Nino kept his head buried in the menu.

"My buddy at Bergdorf-Goodman. I didn't give him any details but I gave him a heads up that I'm going to want to meet with his boss."

"Good for you."

"Hey, look at me," Mickey said.

Nino lowered the menu.

"I need the designs from Armand. I can't keep going the way I am. I've got a window here. We've been over this. There is no risk. Now do you have the designs or not?"

Nino knew Mickey perhaps better than anyone. The desperation that had been in Mickey's voice during the previous week's requests for the designs was gone. He was calm, focused. If pressed, Nino had to admit, he couldn't find any real flaws in Mickey's plan.

"I'm supposed to meet the guy out at Idlewild this afternoon."

This was not a "no" from Nino. Mickey's heart beat faster but his outward appearance was calm.

"Great. I'll meet you right after."

"No. I've got other stuff I've got to do then."

A great salesman knows when a deal is ready to close. There might be a few last objections to overcome, the final struggles of the salesman's prey. Mickey's job at that point was to make the "buy" decision easy for his customer.

"Okay. I'll meet you first thing in the morning. Where do you want to meet for breakfast?"

"Jesus, Mick, twenty grand. I've never made a loan this big. If you can't pay this back..." Nino didn't even want to imagine the consequences.

"Twenty grand is a drop in the bucket to Bergdorf's. I figure their order will be for at least fifty. Minimum. Believe me, I've done the math."

Nino stared at Mickey, checking one last time for a chink in his armor. Mickey stared back matching Nino's intensity.

"All right, Fuck Head, you're in the fashion business."

NINE

~⌒~

Nino took a cab to Idlewild, making sure he arrived early. He wanted to get a look at the new jetways that allowed passengers to walk directly onto a plane in Pan Am's futuristic Worldport terminal.

The transfer of the designs went smoothly. Nino met the Frenchman outside the Panorama Room restaurant that overlooked the concourse. Few words were spoken when Nino handed over the envelope his father had given him. Both men assumed the cash in the sealed envelope was the agreed upon amount. The Frenchman got his cash. Nino got the briefcase containing the designs for Armand's new line of women's wear.

The return cab ride had Nino arrive at The New School in time to watch Peter Ivanofsky rush down the street making his late-as-usual dash to class. Seeing the big Russian, shirttail out, weaving between anyone not walking at a normal New Yorker's frantic pace, made Nino smile. He had enjoyed the time he spent with Ivanofsky. He liked the guy.

"Nino, good to see you," Ivanofsky panted.

"Yeah, you too. You got this week's payment?"

"Yes, I do," Ivanofsky said, much to Nino's surprise. A day earlier, a long shot filly at Aqueduct had confirmed an Ivanofsky hunch and paid enough to ease his financial woes for at least a week. He was convinced that this was surely the beginning of a hot streak.

"Let me ask you something," Nino said as Ivanofsky peeled off his weekly payment plus an additional two hundred dollars of principal from a wad of bills. "Brain chemistry. How come you haven't done something about yours?"

"You have never heard the saying, 'Physician heal thyself'?"

"No."

"This dilemma, knowing what to do but not being willing to do it, this is a struggle we all get to enjoy. I'll explain more. Come. Come to class."

Ivanofsky put his arm around Nino's broad shoulders and the two walked into The New School.

∽

Uptown, Tippy Daniels was putting the finishing touches on her make-up. For the first time in a long time she didn't mind what she saw in the mirror.

That morning she stood in the same bathroom staring at the open medicine cabinet. There, along with the varied and sundry over-the-counter meds, was her bottle of Librium. She took the bottle from the cabinet and held it in her hand. She read the recommended dosage, "one 25 mg capsule, four times daily". She opened the bottle and poured the entire contents into her palm. There were close to thirty pills in her hand. She looked at the pills and then looked at herself in the mirror. She hardly recognized herself. There were dark circles under her eyes. Her hair was matted. She looked old and tired. This was not the life she had hoped for. This was not a life worth living. Suddenly, an unexpected sneeze scattered the handful of pills all over the bathroom floor. The energy and desire to pick them up just wasn't available. She halfheartedly tried to push the pills together with her foot. Even that required more energy than she could muster so she shuffled back to bed. When Tippy awoke a few hours later she lay in bed thinking about the lack of life she was living. She considered her choices: Continue inhabiting a world of mental fog and confusion or...or what? Take the entire bottle at once and end it? Enough hours had passed since taking her last dose of Librium that a few extra neurons were still firing.

Ending her life was not an attractive option. But neither was living life as it was. She wondered if the pharmacy had possibly made a mistake and given her medication that was the wrong strength. Or perhaps she was unusually sensitive or had some kind of allergy to this particular medication. Either way, she couldn't imagine that other people were having the same trouble functioning while under a doctor's care. Lying there she wondered if she could muster the wherewithal to retake control of her life. What would happen if she stopped taking the drug that she was convinced was making her so dysfunctional? It would upset her mother. This would be nothing compared to Mummy's upset over marrying Mickey. She could live with that. Mickey? He wasn't happy with how she was now. She knew that. Surely he'd welcome a return of her old self. Dr. Collins? What if the old medicine man didn't really know how a young woman should feel? What if he was completely wrong in his diagnosis? What if she had given him too much power over her life? He had thrown her into this mental gulag simply because she didn't want to have a baby. That thought reminded her that she had not yet taken her daily dose of The Pill.

Back in the bathroom she opened "her drawer", the one with emery boards, eyelash curlers, and feminine hygiene products. Tucked safely in the back of the drawer was the handy dispenser that helped women keep track of The Pill's required cyclical routine. After making sure she had not missed any days, not an easy feat with her current mental acuity, she swallowed a pill and returned the remainder to the all-the-way-in-the-back-under-the-Tampons-he'll-never-look-there hiding place.

Tippy shifted her weight and felt something under her bare foot. She had not yet dealt with the spilled Librium. While down on her hands and knees, picking up each capsule individually and placing it back in the vial, the thought occurred to her: why not just sweep them all up and flush them down the toilet? If the only reason she was taking them was to change her feelings about procreation, then they weren't working. She did remember, however, that Dr. Collins had warned her about all together stopping her dosage too suddenly. He had described withdrawal symptoms that gave her flashbacks to high school health class warnings about the dangers of heroin. "Use it once, you're hooked," her gym teacher had said. The teacher then gave a horrific account of the potential withdrawal symptoms experienced by addicts if they didn't get their required fix.

Tippy rested her head on the cool toilet seat as she groped behind the commode for the last of the lost pills. Got it. As she rose, she made a decision: on this day she would not take the prescribed four capsules. Today, and for the next few days, she would take only three. And then she would cut down to two per day. And then one per day followed by freedom.

A mid-morning dose had Tippy back in bed lacking the will to dress for the day. But by late afternoon, instead of taking the next prescribed round, she decided to ride a slight increase in energy and brain function and be alive as she could be when Mickey got home from work.

Make-up in place, Tippy was just zipping up her dress when she heard Mickey close the apartment door. She took one more look at herself in the mirror. It still wasn't the old Tippy, but she looked better than she had in weeks.

Mickey was more than pleasantly surprised when Tippy came out of the bedroom. He assumed that the joy he felt in anticipation of getting the new designs from Nino would be dampened by Tippy's never ending malaise. Seeing her look fresh, and dressed, and smiling made an already great day better.

"Hey, Tip, what's going on?"

She hesitated for a moment. Not because her thoughts had slowed. On the contrary. The distance that had grown between them made her cautious. "I thought we could go out to dinner."

"Great. What are you in the mood for?"

"I don't know. Steak?" The suggestion was more than a simple choice of cuisine. Johnny Fine's Steak House was one of their favorite haunts. They had spent many a romantic dinner at a quiet table for two.

"Perfect. Let's eat."

Tippy found enough energy to allow them to walk the ten blocks to Fine's and enjoy an unusually warm fall night. While waiting on a corner for a light to change, a real effort for Mickey who instinctually wanted to dash across every street, weaving through honking cross-town traffic, he took her hand. Along the way they ran into one of Tippy's college sorority sisters. It had been over a year since Tippy and Mickey had seen Audrey and her husband Chad when they all shared a table at the wedding of another sorority sister. The two couples had enjoyed each others' company. They had all laughed, and danced, and caught up on lives lived since college graduation. Chad reported that he was already a junior partner at his father's law firm. Nepotism had nothing to do with his rapid accent through the firm's ranks he assured the others with a self-deprecating laugh.

Tippy was most interested in Audrey's life as she had managed to snag a job as an assistant editor at The Village Voice. Audrey's days sounded so much more fulfilling than Tippy's which were spent wondering if she would ever rid herself of an unsatisfying void. The evening ended with empty promises of getting together soon.

There wasn't much time for catching up when the two couples re-united on their chance meeting. Tippy and Mickey were both anxious to enjoy a rare night out. Audrey and Chad were not merely on a stroll. They were on a mission. The only way they could get their two-month-old baby, Chad Junior, to stop his nightly, relentless, colic fueled tantrums was a thirty block, rain or shine hike. Chad Junior had just dozed off when the couple stopped to chat with Tippy and Mickey. With his pram no longer providing the soothing motion he required, Chad Junior awoke and resumed his wailing. Audrey's rocking of the baby buggy was no substitute for the constant pace Chad Junior preferred. His renewed screaming provided the soundtrack for what would be a very brief conversation jam-packed with new-parent clichés.

"Having a baby is the most wonderful thing." Audrey

"It changes your life. But in a good way." Chad

"I just hope we get to sleep again someday." Audrey with too much desperation to be hidden by her giggle.

"It changes your life. But in a good way." Chad re-spewing what had become his mantra.

Tippy asked Audrey if she was back to work at The Village Voice.

"No, those days are over. Now my job is taking care of little Chad."

"Do you miss it?" Tippy asked.

"Sort of. It was a great job."

"I can imagine," Tippy said. "I'd love a job like that."

Audrey asked, "Are you looking?"

Before Tippy could answer, Chad Jr. ratcheted up his wailing.

"Sorry, got to keep moving or he'll never stop," Audrey said while adding a snarl towards Chad Jr.

"It changes your life. But in a good way." Chad added, unable to hide a look of resentment as he pushed the buggy up to speed.

While waiting for their entrées to arrive, Mickey told Tippy the source of his excitement; he was attempting something new at work. He would no longer just be making housecoats. He would be forging into the world of designer fashion. He of course avoided telling her how this new opportunity came about. Using stolen designs obtained from his mob-associated best friend didn't have the ring of divine inspiration that the story deserved.

"Well, that explains a lot," Tippy said.

"What do you mean?"

Tippy averted her eyes and toyed with her napkin. "The past few months, you've worked late so many nights. You go on those long walks by yourself when you say you need to think. You've seemed so distant." Her mouth felt suddenly dry. She wasn't sure if she wanted to continue. She took a sip of water. "I figured that you were just trying to get away from me. You know, because of the way those damn pills make me feel. That it was my fault. That maybe you didn't love me anymore. I didn't know what to think."

Mickey reached across the table and took her hands in his. "Tippy, no. Of course I love you." He meant it. And accepting Tippy's theory of his distant behavior was certainly easier than admitting his affair with Charlotte.

"I'm not going to be taking the Librium much longer. I want the old me back. I'm sure you do too. Things are going to be different."

"They are, Tip. They're going to be great."

Mickey's excitement and Tippy's hope for reclaimed clarity made for the best time they had shared in what seemed to be ages. Tippy dared to have a glass of wine even though it was against doctor's orders. Mickey had more than one glass, a lot more, and was still a bit past tipsy by the time they got home.

Tippy couldn't wait to get out of her girdle which had been digging into her stomach since half way through dinner. She slipped into a shortie nightgown that was trimmed in lace. The revealing lingerie had been a gift from Mickey early in their marriage. Her modesty and the fact that she wasn't comfortable sleeping in it had prevented her from ever wearing it. She decided that tonight she would wear it for him.

"You really look pretty tonight," Mickey said as she joined him in bed.

They were both nervous. It had been more than a month since they had shared any intimacy – longer than a couple in their twenties would normally allow. They kissed.

"It changes your life. But in a good way," Mickey whispered, echoing Chad's claims of happiness from earlier in the evening. Mickey mistakenly thought that the return of Tippy's life force meant that whatever drugs she was taking were finally working. "Let's change our lives. But in a good way."

The lovemaking was over in a matter of seconds, to the surprise and disappointment of both of them.

"Maybe you just had too much wine," Tippy said in an effort to make Mickey feel better.

"That has to be it," Mickey said, although he didn't believe that was it. Surely this was his psyche punishing him for his dalliances with Charlotte. The affair had poisoned the water.

Laying there he once again swore to himself that he would end the affair. Things would get back to normal. Better than normal. His life was about to change at work and at home. He would be proud of what he was doing at work. And at home? His thought: they should start a family. It changes your life. But it a good way.

Her thought: I did take my birth control pill this morning, didn't I?

TEN

Nino sat quietly, nursing a cup of coffee while reading Ivanofsky's *Addiction: Mechanisms For Recovery,* ignoring the busy breakfast crowd at Katz's Delicatessen. He was nearly finished reading the technical tome, an accomplishment he intended to achieve before his next meeting with the Russian psychologist. The briefcase with the stolen designs sat on the floor nestled against his leg.

When Mickey sat down Nino quickly closed the book and slipped it onto his lap. The look on his face was one of embarrassment. Reading some ill-gotten porn, or worse, was more easily explained than his sudden interest in the scholarly study of psychology. He wasn't even sure how he felt about his new interest. He certainly didn't want to have to explain it to Mickey. Fortunately, Mickey had only one thing on his mind as he sat down.

"Do you have them?"

"Yeah, I got 'em. But I wish I felt better about this."

"So do I, Nino. Because I don't know what the hell you're still worried about."

"Really? Maybe you'll figure it out in a couple of weeks when it's time for your first payment on twenty grand. And maybe, just maybe, you're going to tell me you don't have it. Then you'll really know what I'm still worried about."

"Jesus Christ, you're unbelievable. It would be nice if you had a little faith in me. You know? You should be happy for me because I'm finally doing what I want to do."

"Fine. I'm thrilled. But if you really want to be a designer, maybe you should design something." Nino reached under the table and pushed the briefcase over to Mickey. "Here you go. Make all your dreams come true."

Forced small talk, a wolfed down order of lox, onions, and eggs, and Mickey was off to buy the better goods needed for the samples he would show at Bergdorf-Goodman. Nino ordered another cup of coffee, re-opened his book, and dove back into his study. His first loan collection of the day would have to wait.

It was almost noon by the time Mickey got to T&T. A concerned Charlotte McKinney met him on the factory floor.

"Where have you been? The buyer from Kreski's called three times. He wants to know when they're getting the replacement goods on all the pieces we had to recall." Charlotte's tone that suggested the world was coming to an end. She moved closer to Mickey, closer than what would normally be appropriate in a working environment, close enough for him to get a whiff of her scent. Then, in what she thought was an enticing whisper, but was closer to a nasal scream to be overheard in the midst of the factory din, she proclaimed, "And I was starting to worry about you." She punctuated her concern by surreptitiously brushing her hand against his leg.

Her touch excited him. His previous night's vow of renewed marital fidelity evaporated. Damn it. What was it about this woman? When Mickey faced Charlotte who was sporting what she thought was the most provocative of smiles, a large black piece of raisin, the remnant of a mid-morning coffee break cruller, lodged between her front teeth, brought him back to the moment.

"Everything is fine," he said. Stepping back from her hormonal force field he added, "I've got a few things I've got to take care of in the office. I don't want to be disturbed."

"Does that mean what I think it means?" Charlotte asked, hoping that Mickey was planning a quickie on his desktop.

"No. It means I don't want to be disturbed. No calls. Nothing."

Mickey entered his office and locked the door behind him. He lowered the window shade blocking anyone's view. He carefully placed the briefcase on his desk. He took a step back and pushed up his sleeves as if he was preparing to do a magic trick. After a deep breath, Mickey slowly snapped open the latches on the briefcase with the same care one would use if opening a treasure chest. He took out a stack of papers and began to spread them out on the desk. There were designs and sketches. The designs outlined the technical specifications and were the actual patterns for the dresses. The sketches gave a glimpse of true fashion masterpieces. After looking at each of the sketches numerous times, he sat down, got the phone number for Bergdorf-Goodman from information, dialed, and got connected to his old associate Barry O'Brien.

"Barry, it's Mickey Daniels. How ya doing?" Mickey didn't wait for an answer. "Listen, Barry I need that favor. I'm ready to show your buyer that new line of upscale ready-to-wear. I promise you, she's going to love it."

Mickey framed the request as a favor but he already knew that Barry O'Brien would oblige. Back in the days when they were both at Gimbel's, where Barry was an assistant buyer and Mickey was his assistant, Barry was accused of taking kickbacks from salesmen who wanted access to Barry's boss. And although Mickey knew of the illegal goings on, when upper management questioned him during their investigation of O'Brien's illegal dealings, Mickey swore up and down that Barry O'Brien was not the kind of guy who would do anything the company would consider improper nor had he witnessed any such behavior. Barry O'Brien owed Mickey. Now it was time to pay him back.

"No problem, Mickey. Like I told you, I can get you in. It's going to be about three months though. My boss has all her buying trips already lined up for next season."

"That's not going to work, Barry. I need to show her my goods before she blows her budget. You've gotta make this work. This will make us even."

Mickey didn't need to re-hash the details of O'Brien's criminal past. There was a debt to be honored.

"I'll get you in next Wednesday morning. Be here at nine. But it's going to be tight. You won't have much time."

O'Brien had no idea just how tight the proposed schedule would be. Mickey would have to have samples for an entire line made in a week.

For a moment he considered returning the designs to Nino. No. He would find a way to get it done.

"I'll see you next Wednesday."

Mickey placed the stack of designs and sketches back into the briefcase and strode to the large cutting table where Myron Friedman, electric cutting knife in hand, was about to cut back panels from a stack of fabric. Friedman, who according to Mickey's best guess had to be at least a hundred and fifty three years old, had worked at T&T ever since Mickey's grandfather founded the company. Friedman adjusted his yarmulke and prepared to make a cut when Mickey pulled the plug on the cutting knife, and in one felled swoop, pushed the neatly stacked layers of fabric that Friedman had prepared off to the side.

"Vat are y'do-ink?" Myron whined with his thick Austrian accent.

"Making room so you can cut some goods, Myron. I need some samples. I've got an appointment next week at Bergdorf-Goodman," Mickey said proudly.

"Right. The day they let you into Bergdorf-Goodman, is the day they make me Grand Marshall of the Saint Patrick's Day parade," the old Jew said with a chuckle.

"Well get your shillelagh ready, old man. Because at nine A.M. next Wednesday I'm meeting with the young misses buyer."

"How'd you talk your way in to Bergdorf's?" Charlotte asked with a bit more surprise in her voice than Mickey would have liked.

"Yeah. What's a fancy shmancy place like that want with what we make?" Myron wanted to know.

"We don't make what we make anymore," Mickey announced. He swung the briefcase on to the cutting table. He called out to Leroy Johnson, the shipping clerk who was standing nearby.

"There's a bolt of fabric, good stuff, wool blend, on the top rack. Get it down, please.

The clerk climbed the ladder to fetch the bolt of fabric – the good stuff – not the crap you use for housecoats – a few yards of fancy that Mickey had purchased years earlier not knowing for what – but knowing that some day he'd make something that required a warp and a woof that was soft enough to die for – a fabric loomed by the gods.

"Wow," was all Charlotte could manage as she admired the sketches.

Myron examined one of the patterns. "Where did you get these?" he asked, already suspicious.

"I did them," Mickey replied.

Myron gave Mickey a "who are you kidding' look over his glasses.

"What?" Mickey asked innocently.

"Nothing," Myron said. "I guess I need my shillelagh again."

"Can you make them, Myron? I'm going to go out and buy some more goods. We have to make the entire line. Can you get this done in a week?"

Myron spread one of the patterns on the table. As he examined the drawing, slowly moving his fingers over the translucent design paper, tears began to well up in his eyes.

"Are you okay, Myron?" Charlotte asked, placing a hand on his shoulder.

Myron did not look up from the table. Speaking quietly he said, "In Vienna, my brother and I had our own shop. My brother, he was... well...a *bisel faygel*. But, what an artist? The gowns he designed – fabulous. I sewed every stitch. They were worn by royalty. When it was time to leave, he stayed. He said his special friend, he worked for the mayor, he would protect him." Myron closed his eyes and took a deep breath. Then he looked to Mickey. "You want to know if I can make these? I can make these like nobody else."

Eleven

Each day Tippy felt more human. Her self-prescribed withdrawal plan was working. She was already down to two Librium pills per day without any noticeable withdrawal symptoms. She swallowed one pill at bedtime so she could sleep through the side effects, then a half in the morning and another half mid-afternoon. Her mind still wasn't quite back to full speed ahead, but she felt a thousand times more clearheaded than she had in months. This morning she would skip the half a pill wanting all her faculties working as close to their peak as possible. She had taken an early morning shower and put on make-up while Mickey slept soundly. She wore an un-ironed housecoat, however, hoping that Mickey would not notice her re-discovered vitality. Not this morning. As soon as Mickey would leave the apartment, she would get dressed and head off to her first job interview. No sense getting Mickey involved until she actually got the job.

The possibility of a job had popped up a few days earlier. As Tippy's mental cloud was giving way to newfound clarity, she got a phone call from her new-mom friend, Audrey. With Chad Jr. screaming in the background, Audrey mentioned that she had been offered a job as an assistant to famed author Norman Mailer. Audrey couldn't take the job because now she was a full-time mom. But she remembered that Tippy seemed interested in that kind of work. Audrey recommended that Mr. Mailer meet with her friend Tippy who might be perfect for the job. An interview was arranged.

Now Tippy needed to get Mickey out of the apartment so she could get ready for her interview. Unfortunately he wasn't moving. He was absentmindedly doodling on a napkin. Doodling dresses while envisioning his upcoming sales call at Bergdorf-Goodman.

"Are you going to work today?" Tippy asked.

The question brought Mickey back to the moment. He looked at his watch and then at Tippy. He couldn't help but notice she looked good. Very good.

"Maybe not. Maybe we should go back to bed," he said, adding a wink.

"Can't."

"Why not?"

"You know." In Tippy's mind a lie without specificity was no lie at all.

"Plumbing problems?"

She simply shrugged, suggesting what else could it be.

"Okay, but you owe me one," Mickey said. He then kissed her, gave her a pat on the ass, stepped back and looked at her in her T&T housecoat. "We should get you some sexy underwear or something."

She laughed. "What are you talking about? Go to work."

One more quick kiss, a "Woof," and he was gone.

Tippy quickly rummaged through her closet looking for the perfect job interview dress. A navy blue pencil dress would be conservative enough for someone of Norman Mailer's stature, yet still show enough of her shape. Once dressed, she got a cab to the brownstone where she was to meet the famed author.

By 1960 Mailer was already a prolific literary giant known for his great, although very opinionated, intellect. The idea of working with a man capable of creating novels, non-fiction, screenplays, and stage plays was both frightening and exciting.

His secretary led Tippy into the inner office where Mailer sat behind his massive desk. Cluttered with manuscripts in various stages of completion, the centerpiece was an Underwood typewriter with the artist at work.

The secretary sat Tippy across from Mailer who, once introduced, got right down to business.

"You don't have any babies, do you?" Mailer asked. "Audrey says she can't take the job because she's had a baby. Do you have one? Are you going to have one?"

The questions made Tippy laugh out loud, surprising her and Mailer. It put them both at ease.

"No. No babies anytime soon. God, no."

"Good. I'm thinking of running for mayor and I need someone to help with the campaign. Do you like politics?"

Before Tippy could answer Mailer's secretary stuck her head in the door. "Sorry to bother you but Mark Goodson is on the phone."

"Who?"

"Mark Goodson. Producer. What's My Line? He says it's important."

"I'm sorry, I have to take this," he said. Before answering the phone he proudly added, "I'm going to be the mystery guest on this week's show."

He picked up the receiver. "Mark, Norman. How are you?"

Tippy was already impressed by Mailer's literary achievements. But the possibility of working for a man who was going to be the mystery guest on What's My Line, the hit quiz show, well there was something that might finally impress her parents.

Tippy could not hear what Mark Goodson had said, but whatever it was, it put Norman Mailer in a foul mood.

"That's ridiculous," he bellowed. "You're the producer. Surely you can say that you want me on the show."

Tippy wasn't sure what to do. Look at him? Not look at him? She decided that watching him on the call would be a show of strength.

"Who wants me off the show? Is it Killgalan? It is, isn't it? It's that right wing bitch."

Dorothy Killgalan, was a regular panelist on the show whose politics were on the opposite end of the political spectrum from a liberal Democrat like Mailer. He despised every thing about her.

"This is a load of crap, Mark, and you know it," Mailer said just before slamming down the phone. His tirade continued with an explanation to Tippy.

"He says it's the network. He says they don't want me on the show because of...well I had a minor run in with the law a few weeks back."

Tippy was aware of the minor run in. Everybody in New York City was aware of the minor run in. Besides being known for his literary prowess, Norman Mailer was known as someone who loved to drink, often to excess. One night, while roaring drunk, he stepped into the middle of Sixth Avenue to hail a taxicab. Unfortunately it was not a cab he waved at while standing in the middle of the major thoroughfare, bringing traffic to a screeching halt. It was a police car. Mailer was arrested for public drunkenness. The next morning a picture of a handcuffed Mailer was front-page news in all of New York's papers. Most political aspirants would recognize the episode as the end of their viability as a candidate. Not someone with Mailer's enormous ego. He figured that New Yorkers would identify with him as a regular guy, a guy just like them, who happened to be drunk enough to think a police car was a taxicab. He may have been right.

"He says it's the network, but I bet it's Killgalan. God damn Republican," Mailer said more to himself than to Tippy. Then he turned to her. "My god, you're not a Republican, are you?"

"I'm a white Protestant raised in Connecticut. What do you think?"

He smiled. Mailer liked her honesty but not the idea of having a Republican working on his Democratic campaign. But Tippy quickly added, "On the other hand, I married a Jew from Brooklyn who works in the garment district and you know those people are practically communists."

He laughed. "I guess if they'll have you. Tippy, I'd like you to be my administrative assistant in the campaign if I run. Do you think you can do that?"

The candidacy of young John F. Kennedy had made the world of politics suddenly sexy. She had no idea what the job of administrative assistant would entail, but the possibility of being in the New York political scene was too exciting.

"I've never worked on a campaign but I promise I'll work hard."

"There's a party for me tonight – some friends, some potential supporters. We're going to decide if I should actually do this. As soon as I've made the decision, I'll let you know. If I run, you've got the job."

TWELVE

Nino had one more collection to make before lunch and he wasn't looking forward to it. The doorman, the concierge, and the desk staff of the posh Sherry-Netherlands Hotel all avoided eye contact as Nino crossed the lobby to the elevators. They were all well aware that Nino showed up each Thursday, like clock work, and went up to Edgar Keeling's suite for reasons unknown. What they did know was that Nino certainly seemed like a guy with whom you did not want to make eye contact.

Edgar Keeling was in the oil import business. In the early 1930's, when the adventurous Edgar was in his twenties, he traveled to the Arabian Peninsula. Americans were a rarity in that part of the world and Edgar's presence was made known to Abdul-Aziz Al Saud, the warring tribal chief who had become the first king of modern Saudi Arabia. Edgar was summoned to the palace where he and the king got along famously. The pair remained friends until the king's death in 1953. During that time, as the king's fabulous wealth grew with the development of Saudi Arabia's vast oil riches, Edgar was able to parlay his friendship into vast riches of his own. Oil money had made him more than enough to allow him permanent residence in the penthouse suite of the Sherry-Netherlands.

When Nino arrived at the penthouse, the door was, as always, ajar. Nino shook his head in disgust before knocking.

"Edgar, are you in there?"

There was no answer. He knocked again.

"Edgar, do we have to do this every time?"

Again, there was no response. Nino pushed the door open and entered the suite. Keeling was seated on the couch in the suite's living room. The fifty-five-year-old tycoon, neatly dressed in his silk smoking jacket, didn't bother getting up when Nino entered.

"Nino, what are you doing here?"

"Look, the first couple of times this was okay. But now, this is fucking crazy. Just give me the money."

"I don't have the money."

"Why did you even take the loan? Obviously you and your oil business are making a shit load of money. Come on. Just pay me so I can go."

"I don't have the money. You better do what you have to do."

"I'm not going to hit you, Edgar. I'm not. So come on."

"I swear. I don't have it. Please don't hurt me."

"How do you think this makes me feel, huh? You think I like doing this?"

"Just give me another week. Please."

"Jesus Christ, you are nuts." Nino walked to the couch, grabbed Keeling by the lapels and roughly got him to his feet. "Give me the money."

"Please, believe me. I don't have it," Keeling pleaded.

Nino punched Keeling hard in the stomach. He doubled over and fell to the floor.

"Give me the money or I'll fucking kill you." Rage was building in Nino. He hated this song and dance.

"I don't have it," Keeling wailed.

Nino took Keeling by the hair and pulled him up.

"Give me the money."

"I wish I could."

Nino slapped him across the face.

"The money."

"I just need a week."

Nino slapped him again. Keeling began to weep. Again Nino slammed his fist into Keeling stomach sending him to the floor.

"Come on, Edgar. I gotta go. I'm meeting a buddy for lunch. He hates it when I'm late."

From the fetal position Keeling groaned, "It's in the top drawer."

Nino walked to the desk that sat in a vestibule overlooking Central Park. He opened the top drawer and took out an envelope with his name on it. He didn't bother looking inside. He knew the money was in there just like it always was. "You are one sick fuck, Edgar," Nino said on his way out of the suite.

"See you next week," Keeling moaned from the floor.

Nino hailed a cab and headed down to Park Avenue and 28th Street to the Belmore cafeteria. The Belmore was a hangout for cab drivers but Mickey also liked to meet there for lunch. For Mickey, because of Tippy's lack of cooking skills, the Belmore was the closest thing he got to home style cooking. It was convenient for Nino since he often had cab drivers who owed his father money.

Mickey was already at a table with his meatloaf and mashed potatoes and gravy when Nino sat down. All Nino had on his tray were four pieces of apple pie.

"You call that a lunch?"

"I call this the four pieces of pie I'm going to eat before I go back for more pie. You don't know what kind of day I'm having," Nino said as he practically inhaled the first slice of pie. "I don't know how much longer I can do this, Mick. Beating people up. Constantly in an agitated state. I'm not sure it's good for me."

"Good for you? Whose job is good for them? You're the boss' son. You got security. Besides, what would you do instead?"

"Something other than this. I don't know. Turns out, I don't have a lot of skills."

The two sat quietly for a moment while Mickey carefully folded the potatoes into the gravy.

Nino stuffed another half piece of pie into his mouth before asking, "What's doing with the Bergdorf deal?"

"Myron's putting together the samples. You won't believe what they look like. Gorgeous."

"They're going to be done in time?"

"Yeah. No sweat. He's got two days. We're right on schedule."

A cab driver with a love for back-alley craps games walked by and dropped an envelope next to Nino who didn't even bother to look up. The cabbie was a good customer.

"If there were more like that one, I could handle this job," Nino said, as he slipped the envelope into his jacket pocket. "How's Tippy doing?"

"She's good. I don't know what, but something is going on. It's like all of a sudden she's coming back from the dead."

"How come?"

"Who knows? Maybe the pills she takes are finally starting to work. But this morning at breakfast, she was still acting a little weird. You know, not all the way back."

"So did you say goodbye to Charlotte?"

"Almost."

"Almost? What does that mean?"

"It means I'm trying. I'm just waiting for the right time."

"You want my advice? You're addicted to this chick. You've said it yourself. She's got your brain chemistry messed up."

"What's that supposed to mean?"

"That there is no right time. If you're going to break this thing off, you gotta just do it."

"That's your advice?"

"Yeah. I'm telling you, Mick. Get it over with. If you can't do it yourself, go see a psychologist or something."

"Do what?"

Nino was not prepared to discuss his newfound interest in the social sciences. He ended the conversation with, "You just gotta do what you just gotta do."

Two more payments from cabbies, two more pieces of pie, and Nino left for his next appointment. He had to get all the way downtown to meet with Professor Peter Ivanofsky.

Ivanofsky's office door was open when Nino arrived. Nino closed it behind him.

"Nino, what are you doing here? I expected to see you tonight in class."

"Yeah, well I've got some other stops downtown so I figured I get this done."

"Are you not coming tonight? I've watched you in class. I think you like it."

"It's okay. Yeah. But I'm here now for the money. You've got this week's payment?"

"Actually I do not. I could tell why but the fact that it has to do with a horse that did not perform as anyone might have expected. I will save you from the details."

Nino took a moment to collect himself before saying, "Get up."

"Nino, there is no need for this. You know I will have the money next week. And tonight, you should come to class anyway."

"Get up."

Nino's menacing tone was enough to get Ivanofsky to slowly rise out of his chair.

Nino looked Ivanofsky directly in the eye. "Okay, so I've been reading your book about addiction. And you're saying that when somebody starts an addiction it's fun. It's exciting. Doesn't matter what you're addicted to: heroine, gambling, hookers, whatever. But then at some point, it's not so much fun anymore. But you can't stop. You know, like you and the gambling."

"I love it too much."

"It's the same with me and the smacking people around. Not the love it part. The addiction part. I think I got addicted. When I first started I liked that I was a tough guy. I liked seeing that fear in someone's face. The look that you've got now. I got to where, deep inside, I was happy to see when people didn't have a payment. I got to smack them around. But lately, I don't know, I don't like to do it. I don't know if it's your book, or what. So I say to myself, 'Okay, Nino, you're addicted. What are you going to do about it? How about if I go a whole day without smacking someone around, and see how that feels.' So, yesterday, that's what I did. And you know what, it felt great. So I figured I wouldn't smack anyone around today. You know, one day at a time. But then I had some weird son of a bitch this morning who won't pay me unless I smack him around, and now you're not paying me so technically I'm supposed to smack you around. I don't know what to do."

Before Ivanofsky could say anything, Nino drove his fist into the fat Russian's belly. Ivanofsky fell to the floor.

"All right, how much money do you have?" Nino asked, expecting an answer even though Ivanofsky had not yet been able to breathe.

Nino raised his foot and was about to drop his heel on Invanofsky's nose when the Professor managed to grunt a few words. "Wait. I have a proposition."

"Yeah? What kind of proposition?"

Ivanofsky was still doubled over when he managed to stand. Then, slowly, he straightened up. He offered Nino the chair next to his desk. "Please, sit."

Nino hesitated. What was the Russian up to? Nino sat in the chair. Ivanofsky moved to his chair behind the desk. He took a cigarette and offered one to Nino.

"Forget that. What's this proposition?"

Ivanofsky lit his cigarette and took a huge drag. He held the smoke in while he organized his thoughts. He laid out a plan that he hoped would save his life.

"Okay, we both have a problem. You have grown as a person and no longer like beating up your fellow man. I, because I am weak, have made a foolish loan which I clearly cannot pay," Ivanofsky said.

Nino was losing patience. "You've got exactly two seconds to get to the point."

"What if I could help you solve your problem? If I could do that, will you help me solve mine?"

"The only problem I've got right now is figuring out how much of a beating we're going to need to get the money outta you."

"Please. These threats will not solve anything. Look, Nino, you clearly hate what you do in your work. That is no way for any man to live. But here's what I have noticed: Because of your work, you have real insight into people's emotions. You see people at their worst, when they are begging, or lying."

"So which are you doing now?"

"From just the few times you have been to class I can see that you have empathy. I think you would rather help people than beat them up."

"If you think this is going to get you out of a beating."

"Hear me out. I think you would make a great psychologist. I think you can help people and you'd like doing it. It is a skill you could develop. So I propose that I will get you a masters degree in psychology, allowing you to be a psychologist, if you forgive me the rest of my debt."

"Masters degree? I've never even gotten a regular degree from college."

"If I get a transcript form from Columbia, where I teach during the day, my guess is that in your line of work you may know someone who can create documents that will look authentic and that will say you've done all your course work. You can have all "A's" if you want."

Nino considered this for a moment. "I may know somebody who could do that."

"I will then take the transcript and put it into the files at Columbia. If anyone checks, they will have a record of you. I will also get you a blank diploma. You'll be an Ivy League graduate."

"Yeah, but I won't really know anything."

"Most of it is *yerunda*. I'll tell you what you need to read. You'll be fine."

"Okay, and then what?"

"Then you take my course here at The New School, we create a record that shows you completed this work, and you get your masters."

"You just came up with all this now?"

"In life, when you anticipate a moment like this, which I did, then you should have a plan ready. This will take some work but I think we can do this." Ivanofsky could see that Nino was considering his offer.

"This is a pretty complicated plan."

"This is nothing compared to getting extra toilet paper in Russia. I help you so you don't have to do this work you don't really like, and you charge your other customers a little more here, a little more there, until my loan is satisfied."

"What about a license? Doesn't the state have a test or something that I have to take?"

"This will also be a forgery. You will take my license, like this one on the wall, and have one of your associates copy it. Your patients will see your diploma from Columbia, your master's degree from this fine institution, and your license from the state of New York. The chances of you getting caught are very small. The only time patients really complain to the state is if you fuck them."

"What do you mean, fuck them?"

"Fuck them. Pull your pants down and fuck them. Don't fuck them and no one will know you exist."

"And what if something goes wrong? What if you get caught screwing with the transcripts? What then?"

"Then, business as usual. Then...then you kill me."

THIRTEEN

Waiting for the phone call from Norman Mailer was too stressful for Tippy. This was confirmed the next morning after she poured coffee onto her corn flakes. She decided to take a whole Librium. As the little pill lowered the curtain on her anxiety, she wondered if the job would be too much for her to handle. She didn't have to wonder for long. Mickey returned from the corner grocery with an assortment of Danish and the morning paper. When he threw the paper onto the dinette table she saw the picture on page one. It was a handcuffed Norman Mailer being taken out of a police paddy wagon. This was not a rehashing of his previous arrest. This was new information. She slid the paper toward herself as calmly as she could so as not to raise suspicion. She began reading and quickly learned that during the political get-together the previous evening, Mailer got roaring drunk and stabbed his wife in the heart with a penknife. He did not kill her, but still. New Yorkers had, in the past, put up with some fairly bizarre behavior from their politicians. Evidently, stabbing one's wife in the heart crossed the line for even the staunchest of supporters. There would be no campaign. There would be no job. Tippy sank into her chair. As Mickey wolfed down a cinnamon raisin cruller, he noticed that the spark that had recently returned to Tippy's eyes was suddenly gone again. He didn't take the time to ask if something was wrong. He had his own worries that day. This would be the last day for Myron to complete the samples. Mickey wanted everything to be perfect for his presentation to Bergdorf-Goodman. He was anxious to get to the office.

Once Mickey was gone, Tippy allowed herself a good cry. The job with Normal Mailer had seemed perfect. She hadn't even pursued it. It just showed up on her doorstep. It was as if life knew it was time for her to move on to something new. Now that was gone. There might not be another opportunity. The vision to see a brighter future was dimmed as the Librium took full effect.

By lunchtime Tippy was starting to feel like herself again. It had been a number of days since she had taken a full dose of the mood-altering drug and the morning's experience convinced her that she would not be taking a full dose again. As her mind returned to a more natural state, she realized she was getting hungry. While getting dressed she made a decision. She would not wait for life to present another opportunity for her to go to work. She would actively engage in her pursuit.

～

Ramón Fuentes had a good corner. Every weekday, for five years, ever since he first arrived from Puerto Rico and his cousin Eduardo taught him the ropes, Ramón would set up his Sabrett hot dog cart knowing that business would be steady. Some of the first English words he learned were "One with mustard and kraut and a Yoo Hoo," as he served an endless stream of New Yorkers grabbing a meal on the run. Talking with customers each day, he quickly learned the language. He liked his work, no matter what the weather. He especially liked the people – his regulars who knew him by name and appreciated his happy demeanor and got a kick out the "bon appétit," Ramón served up with each all beef frank.

"Hey, Mrs. Tippy, how you doin'?" Ramón asked Tippy Daniels as she approached the cart. "One or two today?"

"Just one with onions, Ramón," Tippy answered with a sigh. She still wasn't over the missed job opportunity although she had to concede that if Norman Mailer was capable of stabbing his wife in the heart at a party, perhaps working for him wasn't that great an opportunity after all.

She watched as Ramón plucked a hot dog from the propane heated water, put it on a bun, then smothered it with onions swimming in a delicious looking tomato sauce.

"Here you go. Bon appétit."

Tippy took a bite, and with her mouth full asked, "How's your wife doing?"

"She's having a baby," Ramón said while taking an order from the next customer.

"I know that. How is she doing?" Tippy asked slowly thinking Ramón may have misunderstood her question.

"She's having a baby right now." Ramón said with a smile. "How about that?"

Tippy stopped eating. "Right now?" she asked in order to confirm what he had said. "What are you doing here?"

"She'll be okay," Ramón said firmly. It sounded as if he was trying to convince himself as much as Tippy. Even with a good corner, Ramón could not afford to miss a day of selling hot dogs. Taking off in order to pace around the waiting room while his wife gave birth was not an option. "God willing, it will be a long labor and I'll get to the hospital before the baby comes."

"You should be with her." Then, having planted the seed of ambition just hours earlier, an idea began to form. Dealing with clear thoughts still hadn't become her norm. To be safe, she took another bite of hot dog giving her time to evaluate what might be a brainstorm. "Go to the hospital, Ramón. I'll watch the cart so you don't lose any business."

"I can't do that," Ramón said, although Tippy could see that he was touched by the kind offer.

Another wave of clarity came over her. "Ramón, I'm here practically every day. I can do this." Tippy then proceeded to call out, and point out where Ramón kept the, "Dogs, buns, kraut, onions, mustard, ketchup, pretzels, and drinks. I'll be fine."

"But at the end of the day I have to get the cart back," Ramón explained. "How are you going to do that?"

Now Tippy was excited. "I'll do it. Come on. Let me do this. Go be with your wife."

Ramón took a moment to seriously consider the offer then said, "You gotta be here till around five-thirty, you know when the commuters go home for the night. Then you take the cart to fifty-ninth between second and third. There's a garage. You can't miss it. It's the one with all the hot dog carts."

"Don't worry. Go have a baby," she said, bubbling with enthusiasm. She felt alive.

Ramón hesitated, then removed his apron and handed it to Tippy. She quickly put it on before he could change his mind.

He watched as she asked a man in a business suit "What'll you have?"

"Two with mustard and kraut and a Coke," the man said.

Ramón didn't leave until he saw Tippy deftly prepare the hot dogs. Then, after prying off the cap from the Coke on the cart-side opener she handed the man his lunch, smiled broadly, and added a "bon appétit" of her own.

FOURTEEN

Mickey spent most of the day in his office admiring Myron's artistry. The samples were exquisite. He had done some shopping to see what fashions designed by Armand were selling for and did some quick math. Assuming stores were taking the normal keystone markup from wholesale, and considering that each dress was selling for a small fortune, huge sums of cash would soon be headed his way. It wouldn't be long before T&T Fashions was making its last housecoat. Before leaving for the night Mickey gave Myron instructions to stay as late as necessary to complete the samples. Myron could take the next day off if need be, but the samples had to be finished by morning.

Mickey headed for the door with Charlotte falling in behind him.

Looking back over his shoulder, Mickey asked, "Where are you going?"

"My place. Care to join me?" she asked much too loudly.

That stopped Mickey in his tracks. He almost put his hand over her mouth but quickly realized that the noisy factory had made her invitation heard only by him. He did not want to go to her place. His lunchtime confessions to Nino confirmed what he already knew in his heart; he hated himself for cheating on Tippy and had to stop seeing Charlotte and her irresistible unmentionables. Now was the time. His life was about to change. As of tomorrow morning he'd really be in the fashion business. The timing was perfect. He'd make one more visit to her apartment and deliver the news. They'd arrive together so there wouldn't be time for her to slip into something revealing, or enticing, or so silky smooth and sensual to the touch that simply caressing the fabric would qualify as a sexual act. That thought alone made Mickey, although not particularly religious, quickly say a silent prayer that he might find the strength to never see Charlotte in the biblical sense again.

Mickey and Charlotte stood together at the crowded bus stop. He nervously played with a quarter and a nickel, bus fare for both, shaking the coins like a pair of dice.

A clap of thunder announcing an approaching thunderstorm startled Charlotte. She took his arm and snuggled up to him. She felt his arm go limp and he edged away from her.

"Nobody cares, Mickey."

"I care," he said, looking straight ahead as if he weren't with her.

Before the conversation could continue the bus and the rain arrived at the same time. The bus stopped directly in front of Mickey and Charlotte allowing them to get on before the quickly raging downpour soaked them.

Charlotte slipped into an empty seat followed by Mickey. The bus quickly filled to capacity with passengers ranging from damp to drenched from the late afternoon shower. Mickey was already uncomfortable and the fact that very few things in life smell worse than a New York City bus or subway when they are packed to capacity on a hot, wet afternoon didn't make him feel any better.

As the bus moved up Third Avenue, Charlotte began to play with Mickey's fingers. He quickly moved his hand away. She stared at him for a moment before asking, "If the Bergdorf order happens could we take a vacation together?

"A vacation? What the hell are you talking about?"

"I'm talking about us spending some time together. I've got vacation time coming. I want us, the two of us, to go somewhere."

For a moment Mickey thought that this would be the perfect time to tell Charlotte that it was over between them. But he suddenly became aware that the woman standing next to his seat was listening intently to their conversation. He stared at her until she finally looked away.

"A vacation? I shouldn't even be seen with you," Mickey said quietly. "I'm a married man."

"Well, I feel bad when you act so distant. I mean look at you. We're on a bus. You're not going to see anybody on a bus. I just think that if we go away together you'll relax a little."

"I doubt it. I know I'll get caught. We're not going."

They sat without saying a word for a moment or two before Charlotte began to cry. Although she tried her best to contain herself, she began to quietly sob.

"Don't do that," Mickey said while taking her hand. He hoped the gesture would settle her down. It didn't. She spoke through her tears, gasping for air between pleas that grew increasing loud.

"I'm sorry" – gasp – "it's just that I care" – gasp – "about you" – big gasp. "And when I think" – gasp – "that"- gasp – "I'm going to go" – gasp – "through life" – gasp – "without finding my true love" – gasp – gasp – gasp – wail."

Mickey was aware that not only the woman standing next to his seat staring at them, now half the bus wanted to see what was going on.

Mickey put his arm around Charlotte. The move did not stop her noisy outbreak. "Okay, okay. Stop crying. We see about a vacation. We'll figure out something." He knew it was the only thing he could say that would stem the growing tantrum.

"We will?" Charlotte sniffled while wiping her nose with her coat sleeve.

"If the Bergdorf thing goes through," Mickey added as a caveat.

"Oh, Mickey, I love you," Charlotte said much too loudly as she threw her arms around his neck and gave him a big kiss on the cheek.

"Okay. Okay," he said as he peeled her off.

As she regained her composure Charlotte added, "And don't worry. You won't get caught."

Mickey looked around the bus and found his audience was giving him mixed reviews. The younger working girls looked enchanted as if they'd witnessed a wonderful love scene. Most of the men were shaking their heads as if they had just seen one of their own get snookered in the worst way. And the older women, including the old bat standing next to him, looked on in disgust. Mickey forced a smile for Charlotte then gazed out the window as he contemplated how he might get out of the promised illicit get away. It was then, just as the bus stopped for a red light and his thoughts were not of Charlotte but of Tippy and how she'd react to the news that he'd be gone for a few days that he saw her. Tippy! Standing in the rain, looking like a drenched dog, pushing what appeared to be a hot dog cart. Mickey blinked hard thinking his guilt was causing hallucinations. But this wasn't some mirage. That was definitely Tippy and it seemed that she was looking right at him.

Mickey sprung to his feet and began pushing his way to the front of the bus.

"Getting off! Getting off, please!" he called hoping the driver would let him off even though they were not at a bus stop.

As he forced himself by the throng of soggy passengers clogging the aisle he could hear Charlotte calling after him. He made it to the front of the bus before the light changed and it didn't take much convincing to get the driver to open the door.

Mickey bound from the bus just as the light changed. He ran to Tippy as she began pushing the cart through the rain.

"Sweetie, what are you doing?"

"Mickey! Hi!" Her genuine surprise told him that she had probably not seen him on the bus and he could turn his attention to authentic concern.

"Are you okay?"

"You wouldn't believe it. I had the best day. Do you want a hot dog?"

"No, I don't want a hot dog. What is this?

Before she could answer a truck rumbled through an adjacent pothole that had quickly become a small lake sending up a huge spray, soaking Mickey and Tippy to the bone.

"You son-of-a-bitch," Mickey yelled and gave the truck driver the finger. "Come on, Tip, let's get home."

"I've got to get this back to the garage. If you want to go. . ."

"I'm not leaving you." Mickey moved next to Tippy and began pushing the cart. "You're sure you're okay?" he asked just as a second truck passed sending up a wall of water that drenched whatever patch of skin might have avoided the previous soaking.

Tippy just smiled and got the cart moving again. "I'm more than okay. I'm terrific."

∼

Hot showers once they got home had Mickey and Tippy feeling human again. They each wore terry cloth robes, she with a towel wrapped turban-style around her head as they entered the tiny cramped kitchen. Like many New York City apartments, floor space was not wasted on the kitchen and theirs was utilitarian at best. Mickey sat at the small Formica dinette reading his sports page while Tippy opened the freezer. She took out two Swanson's frozen dinners, her version of making dinner.

"Fried chicken or meat loaf?" Tippy asked, generously offering Mickey first choice.

"If the chicken has the apple crisp for dessert, I'll have that," he answered without looking up from the day's baseball news. "How long until dinner? I'm starved."

"These are pretty quick. Once I pre-heat the oven they only take..." Tippy checked the box for cooking instructions. Even though she prepared frozen dinners a few times each week, she never really paid attention. "Forty-five minutes to an hour."

"Maybe we should just order chinks."

"No. That's okay. I feel like cooking." Tippy struck a wooden match and lit the oven's pilot light. She sat across from Mickey who continued to read. She watched him for a moment before letting him know that she had made a decision.

"Mickey, I want to get a hot dog cart."

"A what?" he asked without looking up from his paper.

"I want to get a hot dog cart. I want to go to work."

"Forget it. We're not hot dog cart people."

"I am."

"No you're not. You have all of your fingers. Hot dog guys are always missing at least one finger. I think it's so they can slide the bun in there." Mickey hoped his lighthearted remark would end this request that surely couldn't be serious.

"I want to do this."

"You're not doing this. It's stupid."

"Stupid?"

"Yes. Stupid."

Mickey still hadn't put down the paper and could not feel the searing heat from Tippy's stare. She thought for a moment. Was this idea stupid? Was this just a crazy idea hatched by the remaining molecules of mood altering drugs that had kept her in a perpetual daze? No, in her mind it was not. And why was he still reading that damned paper?

"Are we okay?" she asked.

"What are you talking about? Of course we're okay."

"Look at me, please."

Mickey sighed before putting the paper aside.

"I'm not so sure," she continued. "I mean, everything I say lately, according to you, is stupid."

"I never said that."

"No, but you act that way. I mean, the other night, when we went out to dinner, I said I thought things were my fault. But I don't know. Things are different, Mickey. You know they are. I mean...," she paused, not sure she wanted the answer.

Mickey would normally attempt to finish her sentence. Since her drugs had slowed her mind he found it impossible to wait for her to finish a thought. This time he feared she was headed for a subject he was not prepared to discuss.

"Do you love me? Are you seeing someone else?"

It was just as he feared. Rather than tell the truth, but avoiding the outright lie, Mickey went right into selling mode. "Wait a minute. How do you get from 'don't sell hotdogs' to 'is there someone else'? I just don't want my wife selling hot dogs."

"Well what will you have your wife do? I want to do something?"

Mickey got up from the table and put his arms around Tippy. He pulled her close.

"Look, everything is about to change for us. If it works out..."

Tippy was not in the mood for sweet talk. She held him at arms length.

"What? Then you'll let me work?"

Mickey took a step back.

"How do you think it makes me look if my wife goes to work?"

"Like you really do love me."

With that, Tippy headed to the bedroom leaving Mickey to wonder how and when the lies would end and what to do with his still frozen dinner.

The next morning the Swanson dinners weren't the only things that were still frozen. Having not cleared the air before they went to sleep, the previous night's tension still hung in the air.

Mickey had put on a pot of coffee and they both sat staring at the pot, waiting for it to percolate. It was Tippy who finally broke the silence.

"When I couldn't sleep last night and I was lying there thinking, I was wondering how you couldn't see how happy I was with that hot dog cart yesterday. But then I started wondering, what were you doing on that bus going up Third Avenue? You take the subway home. Where were you going?"

"I was coming home from a customer's."

"Where were your samples?"

Mickey didn't like where this cross-examination was headed. "Okay, you want to know what's going on? I told you the other night that I've been working on some dresses. Better goods. And today I'm showing them at Bergdorf-Goodman. I wanted to surprise you after I make the sale. Okay? So I've got a little on my mind and could do without this today."

"Really, Mickey? Is that what you've been doing?"

"I'm just going downtown to get the samples and then I'm headed up there this morning."

Mickey had not lied. He hadn't explained why he was on that bus either. But he had covered his tracks well enough to allay her suspicions.

"Okay. Well, good luck."

"And about this hot dog cart thing…" Having gotten Tippy off his trail, Mickey hoped to put all the issues from the previous evening's argument to rest.

"We don't have to talk about that now," Tippy said. "You have enough to worry about today."

FIFTEEN

Mickey got to the office and found ten sample dresses neatly hung, a note from Myron wishing him luck, and Nino who arrived bright and early to make sure everything went as planned. Mickey carefully put the dresses in a large garment bag and headed uptown along with Nino.

"You ready to do what you gotta do?" Nino asked as they slid into the back seat of a taxi.

Mickey answered Nino with a wink and instructed the driver to head to 754 Fifth Avenue. Nino checked his watch to make sure it was still ticking as well as to see if they were on time. They had a full twenty-five minutes.

An unannounced slowdown by transit workers, a tactic meant to convince City Hall that slow negotiations on a new contract would not be tolerated, had subways barely running and mid-town Manhattan traffic at a total gridlock. By Forty-third Street Mickey's cab was at a complete standstill. He was not about to miss this meeting. Mickey took a five-dollar bill and handed it to the cab driver before jumping out of the taxi. Nino followed. Mickey began running up Fifth Avenue carrying the huge garment bag. He was doing his best to find his optimum speed without breaking out into a sweat. The pressure of simply making perhaps the most important sales call in his life would be enough to get him perspiring without the additional exertion of this early morning run. Even with his heavy load, Mickey managed to stay ten paces ahead of Nino who followed behind panting heavily. Once they arrived at Bergdorf-Goodman, the ultra high-end department store, the doorman held the door open for Mickey. Nino planted himself on the side of the building to catch his breath and wait to see if he would be celebrating with Mickey or beating him senseless. The doorman gave Nino a disapproving look. Nino returned it with a look so frightening the man went in the store and let any early morning arrivals fend for themselves.

Mickey rushed off the elevator on the eighth floor and half-ran to the receptionist's desk.

Out of breath, he barely managed to say, "Mickey Daniels to see Janet Parker-Simpson."

The receptionist was not about to be rushed. This was Bergdorf-Goodman and a certain amount of polite restraint was expected. But by the time she got out her disregard-laden, "Is she expecting you," Mickey was already headed down the corridor she was supposed to be guarding.

Mickey passed a number of buyers' offices before he found a nameplate that read, "Janet Parker-Simpson". He rushed into the outer office expecting to find his contact, his old Gimbel's co-worker, Barry O'Brien. There was no Barry. Mickey took a deep breath, composed himself, and continued into Parker-Simpson's inner sanctum. There he found Barry O'Brien helping Miss Parker-Simpson pack her briefcase.

"Hey, Barry, how are you?"

"Where the hell have you been?"

Mickey ignored O'Brien's reproach, shifted the massive garment bag to his left hand, extended his right, and walked directly to Janet Parker-Simpson. He hoped he was making the right move. Mickey had never sold to a woman before. He had dealt with women receptionists, secretaries, and assistants, but never the decision maker.

"Janet, Mickey Daniels. Sorry I'm late."

"So am I," she said briefly shaking his hand. She immediately went back to packing. "I have to catch a plane to Paris."

"I only need a couple of minutes. And don't worry. You won't have any trouble getting to the airport." Mickey didn't dare describe the traffic jam that awaited Parker-Simpson. Then, fearing that he might not get this opportunity again, he began unzipping the garment bag as he calmly said, "Wait until you get a look at these."

"I'm sorry. I really can't miss this buying trip. Barry will reschedule you. Although, I don't usually re-see people who have missed an appointment. I have a policy."

"I have a policy too. Once I get my foot in the door I don't take it out," he said with a smile. "Just look at this." With that he pulled a dress from the garment bag.

"I'm afraid not. You see..." Before she could get out her objection, Janet Parker-Simpson, the only female head buyer at all of Bergdorf-Goodman, perhaps the only female head buyer in all of New York, a position she attained because of her exquisite taste and uncanny ability to predict fashion trends, laid eyes on what had to be considered a fabulous dress.

"Oh, my. I like this. The buttons. The neckline."

"Give me ten minutes. They're all this good," Mickey cooed.

"Barry, go grab a cab and hold it."

As O'Brien sprinted out the door, Mickey took out two more dresses. Janet Parker-Simpson slowly ran her hand over the fabric.

"Very nice. They remind me a little bit of Armand. Are you familiar with him?"

"Oh, yeah. He's a big influence on my work." Mickey took the last two samples from his bag.

"Who else have you sold these to?"

"You're the first to see them."

She took one more look at the dresses and asked, "What if I want the whole run? Is that possible? Of course we'd pay extra for an exclusive."

Somehow Mickey kept himself from hollering a war yelp of joy. He stayed outwardly calm.

"Yeah, I sometimes sell exclusives. I suppose I could do that. As long as you're paying extra."

"Not a problem." Then Janet Parker-Simpson noticed the label in one of the dresses.

"What's this label with a picture of The Eiffel Tower?"

"That's just temporary. I was thinking of a label that says, 'Comme

Armand.' That's French for 'like Armand.' It's perfectly legal. I talked with the Federal Trade Commission just the other day."

"Not for our customers. They want the real Armand or not. What's your name again?"

"Mickey Daniels."

"Why don't you have the label read, Michelle Daniel?" she said with a French accent. Then with a giggle she added, "I know it's a little lie. But do you think you could do that?"

"I think I could."

"Okay, then. I've got to run. When Barry comes up he'll go over sizes and stock and give you a purchase order."

She grabbed her briefcase and headed for the door.

"Au revoir, Michelle Daniel," she called out as she ran out.

"Au revoir," Mickey called back before collapsing in Janet Parker-Simpson's chair.

Outside, Nino had made friends with the doorman. They were chatting amicably when Mickey came calmly walking out of the revolving door.

"Well?"

"Give me skin." Mickey extended his hand to Nino.

"You got it?"

"I said give me skin, didn't I."

They both broke out in big smiles as Nino slid his palm across Mickey's.

"What did I tell you?" Mickey said while giving Nino a wink. "From Bergdorf's to the bank."

"Okay. Listen, I gotta take care of some stuff. You go to the bank and I'll meet you later."

As they headed down the street, Nino called back to the doorman, "Hey, Steve-o, enjoy that Rolex."

The doorman checked the time on his newly acquired hot watch before saluting Nino and Mickey.

∼

Tippy did not like what she saw in the mirror. The pearls were all wrong. The white gloves were definitely wrong. She looked like she was going to a Daughters Of The Revolution meeting, not applying for a job selling hot dogs. She didn't own any clothes that were similar to the typical cart vendor. She wondered: what would get her the job? What could she wear that would sell the most hot dogs? She thought back to the business courses she took in college. This was simply a marketing problem. She was aware that whenever she got a hotdog from Ramone, almost all of his other customers were men. It was the same when she substituted for him. It never bothered her but she knew women who felt that it just wasn't lady-like to stand on the corner eating a hotdog. So if the customers were men, what would make a man buy a hotdog from a woman? Then it struck her; the look in Mickey's eyes when he suggested she wear some sexy underwear was the look of real desire. She quickly undressed and began rummaging through her closet. There was a cashmere cardigan sweater she loved but had shrunk. It had become almost form-fitted. Her modesty prevented her from ever wearing it but she couldn't get herself to throw it away. How do you throw away cashmere? She put it on leaving the top few buttons unfastened revealing a hint of cleavage. The sweater went perfectly with a skirt she felt was just a bit too short. High heels wouldn't be sensible if she were on her feet all day standing on unforgiving pavement. They did, however, add the perfect touch to the sweater/skirt combination. She teased her hair, added a bit too much make-up and then re-examined herself in the mirror. Tippy smiled. She looked liked all the "bad" girls seen in B movies about delinquent high school kids. She liked the look. It was a look that just might sell a cart-full of hotdogs.

Jimmy "The Artist" Figaritto examined the Columbia University transcript.

"You want it to look just like this but with your name on it? I don't get it. I can just get rid of this guy's name and type in yours. You'll never know the difference."

"You don't have to get it," Nino said. "This one has to go back where it came from and I need one with my name on it. You can give me the same grades."

"All A's. Impressive. You're a very good student." Jimmy laughed as he used a jeweler's loupe to get a closer look at the paper. If he was going to do the job, it had to be perfect. You don't get a moniker like "The Artist" by doing less than quality work.

"Did you hear about Ralphie Three Shoes?" Jimmie asked while continuing his examination.

Ralphie Bovino was Nino's contemporary. They were schoolmates until the age of sixteen when Ralphie dropped out to spend more time committing pretty crimes. Ralphie's right foot was a full two sizes bigger than his left. At an early age he began buying one pair of shoes, the smaller, less expensive ones to fit his left foot, and stealing a second larger pair for the right. In fact, he only stole the one right shoe that he needed and so the apt nickname, three shoes.

"No. What's he up to?"

"He got busted again for hijacking a cigarette truck. They think he's going away for at least three years."

Nino did not like hearing about fellow travelers being sent to prison. He understood that the odds were in favor of him going to some correctional facility or other at some point in his career.

"When can I get that?" Nino asked.

Holding the page up to the daylight Jimmy asked, "You see this watermark? It's custom. They're trying to be very tricky. Nobody is going to have anything like this in stock."

"So how do we get some?"

"I can make a call. I know a guy."

In Nino's business it seemed like everybody "knew a guy."

"If not. I can probably make it. A lot of work though. Give me two days," Jimmy said.

"How much?"

"Forget it. Just tell your Papa I took care of you."

"My Papa can't know about this one. How much?"

∽

Butch Marotta's mornings were always hell. It was his job to make sure that all 53 Sabrett hot dog carts under his supervision were, on a daily basis, clean – food poisoning is bad for business, fully stocked – you can't make money if you run out of hotdogs, and manned by people capable of plucking an all beef wiener from tepid water, placing it on a bun with the appropriate fixings. That last one sounds easy but it was the toughest. Most of his hotdog vendors were recent immigrants with limited English language skills. Besides that challenge, all of them hated the job in winter when fingers would get cold and stiff from working without gloves. Being on your feet for ten to twelve hours a day (as many hours as it took to sell their daily quota) was no picnic either. This was not a job many aspired to. So as soon as new arrivals gained enough command of the language, they often left for better jobs. Usually without notice which meant carts prepared for the day that sat in the garage. Carts full of food that would spoil and not make any money on that given day. There were five men who hadn't shown up this day and so there were five of those carts sitting in the garage when Tippy Daniels sauntered in to Butch's office.

"Butch?"

He swung around to see who it was. He liked what he saw.

"Maybe. Do I owe you money?" he said with a smile.

"It's me. Tippy Daniels. I met you last night when I brought back Ramone's cart.

"Oh, yeah. I didn't recognize you. You look different."

"That's because I looked like a wet dog last night."

"Yeah. You kinda did. Not today. What can I do for you, Sweet Heart?"

"Well, I'd like a job."

"Yeah, well I'd love to have you around but I already got a bookkeeper. Of course, looking as good as you do, maybe I'll just get rid of the other bookkeeper."

"Thank you but I want to sell hotdogs. I want a cart."

"If you're the bookkeeper we'd get to work together. Very closely together."

Butch had not shaven in two days. The cigar stub he held between his teeth had perhaps been there since the last time he shaved. Butch also must have been eating a good deal of the unsold hotdogs because he was at least a hundred and fifty pounds overweight. His less than subtle come-on was almost laughable. Instead of laughing, Tippy got down to business.

"Let me ask you something, are you on a straight salary or do you make more money based on the number of hotdogs that get sold?"

Although disappointed that she hadn't responded to his amorous invitation, Butch was intrigued by the line of questioning. "Yeah, I get a bonus based on sales."

"Well the way you're looking at me now is how men are going to look at me when I'm selling a whole lot of hotdogs. If I work here in the office, I'm just going to be telling you no over and over again. It's not going to happen. But I can make you a lot of money selling a lot of hotdogs. Do you want the money, Butch?"

Butch was confused. What she said made sense. Still, the idea of a woman selling hotdogs was something he did not relish. His words not mine.

"No. Sorry. We don't hire women for that."

"Why not?"

"It's too tough."

"It wasn't too tough yesterday."

"Yeah, but that was just one day. Really, you don't want this job. It's crazy."

"Believe me, I know crazy. This isn't."

Just then, one of the missing vendors stuck his head in the door.

"Scuse. I late. Still job?" he asked.

"Yeah. Still job. Get out there," Butch said to the man. Then he explained to Tippy, "See, that's what a hotdog vendor looks like."

"Right. And who would you rather buy a hotdog from, him or me?"

Butch looked at the four remaining carts that would not be making any money that day. He looked at Tippy. She was right. Looking as she did, she'd sell a whole lot of hotdogs. She sensed he was softening.

"Butch, who's the legend in the hotdog business?"

"The legend?"

"The legend. If I say cars who's the first person you think of?"

"Henry Ford."

"Right. He's a legend. What about the light bulb?"

"Eli Whitney."

She didn't want him feeling stupid. She let it slide.

"Right. He's a legend. How about hotdogs?"

He had no answer.

"It could be Butch Marotta. You'd be the guy who hired the first woman vendor. And she sells more hotdogs than anybody. And as far as anybody knows, it was your idea. That's our story. You hired that woman. You. Butch Marotta. Legend."

He took a moment picturing himself getting some sort of hotdog award before saying, "Or I could be the guy that made some lady stand out there freezing her rear end off just to sell a few more dogs. Legend. Sorry. It ain't gonna happen."

∽

The banner in front of New York Commercial Bank read, "The Bank That Says Yes." Mickey sat in front of Paul Lewis, as the young banker looked over the Bergdorf-Goodman purchase order. It only took a moment before he began to shake his head and mutter, "No, no, no, no, no."

Mickey reminded him, "You're the bank that says, Yes."

"Today I'm saying No."

"Come on, Paul. You lend me money on orders all the time."

A small time operator like Mickey could not function without some financial institution providing him with liquidity.

"I lend you money on accounts receivable. Stuff you've already delivered. You could blow this money before you even make one dress."

It was more than that. Paul Lewis really only lent Mickey money after he had checked the credit of Mickey's customer. And the bills were paid directly to the bank. He wasn't factoring Mickey's accounts receivables based on his faith and trust in Mickey Daniels.

"That's a purchase order from Bergdorf-Goodman. That's as good as cash," Mickey insisted. "I want a Yes."

"No."

"As I understand it, false advertising is a very serious offense, Paul."

"I've got to get to work, Mickey."

"How am I supposed to buy the goods to make the dresses?"

"I can't. I'm sorry."

"You're sorry? That's the best you can do?"

"Yes. See, I said it."

Nino was already seated on a stool when Mickey entered Phil's Luncheonette, one of a thousand tiny hole-in-the-wall eateries that survive by serving New Yorkers a quick, decent breakfast or lunch.

Mickey took the stool next to Nino who wasted no time in getting down to business.

"Well?"

"Mother fucker," Mickey whispered under his breath.

"What mother fucker? Don't tell me mother fucker."

"He said, 'No.'"

"What are you talking about? I just told my old man it was a go. He said I finally did something right."

"Yeah, well maybe you should go into the bank and convince this guy to give me the money."

"Do you really think that's a good idea, Mick?"

"I don't know what to think."

"Okay, so I take the designs back to my father and tell him what's what. He's always telling me I'm no good at this anyway. He'll get over it."

"Forget it. I'm not giving up on this," Mickey said as he tried to make out the daily specials scribbled on a small blackboard.

Nino put his massive paw of a hand on Mickey's arm and asked,

"How are you going to pay for these designs?"

Before he could answer, Phil (according to his embossed chef's jacket), approached. It was lunchtime and Phil, a Dominican making his American dream come true, was in constant motion. He simply looked at Mickey who knew the routine.

"BLT, toast, bacon crisp, mayo, chips."

Phil called out to his amazing brother, Ricky, a man who never wrote down an order and never got one wrong.

"Mister Ricky, BLT, toast, burn the pig, mayo, chips, please." He then looked to Nino.

"Meat loaf, rye, coleslaw."

"Mister Ricky, a number 4 please."

With that, Phil was gone. Nino just stared at Mickey who needed a plan. And he needed it fast.

"Okay, how about this? There's no risk," Mickey said.

Nino's stare was now so intense Mickey thought one of them might burst into flames.

"No, really, Nino. There's no risk. You lend people money, right?"

"Yeah."

"So you lend me thirty-thousand dollars."

"That's hilarious." Nino said, although he was in no way amused. He turned is attention to a stack of pastries left over from the breakfast crowd.

"Wait, wait, wait. I take twenty thousand and pay for the designs. Right away your father thinks you did good. You sold the designs and you placed a loan for thirty grand. That's what a loan shark is supposed to do, isn't it."

Nino chuckled. "Believe me, you don't want to owe my old man thirty grand. *Madone.*"

"I'm telling you, Nino, there is no risk."

"Would you stop that?"

"Seriously. Look, I take five grand and buy the goods I need to make the dresses. The other five grand I use to make the first payments on the loan to your father. Then once I deliver the goods, Bergdorf's pays me.

I pay you. Bing-a-bang-a-boom. I'm in the fashion business and you're a killer loan shark."

Phil deposited the sandwiches in front of the hungry duo and was gone in a flash.

Nino took a bite of his sandwich and with a full mouth asked, "And you think this can work?"

Mickey, with his mouth just as full answered, "This can't miss."

That night, Nino was still considering Mickey's proposal when he entered Ivanofsky's classroom. He was there to tell the professor that because of the intricate watermark it would be a few days before the forged Columbia University transcript would be ready. It was a message Nino could have easily delivered by phone but, to his surprise, he didn't want to miss Ivanofsky's lecture. This psychology stuff was getting pretty interesting. Nino took his seat. He was already used to the instructor's normally late arrival. He began thinking of how he would propose a thirty thousand dollar loan to his father. Mickey made it sound easy. Nino knew that would not be the case. Before he could come up with a satisfactory plan, the seat next to him became occupied by a young woman. For all his bravura in the world of loan sharking, Nino was painfully shy when it came to women. He couldn't even get himself to take a peek at whoever had planted her self at the next desk. All he knew was that she smelled wonderful. Her perfume was intoxicating. Because of it, he was barely aware of anything Ivanofsky said that night. Although, somehow he managed to correctly answer the two questions posed to him. Both questions had to do with how an addict's behavior affects those around him or her. It was information Ivanofsky's book covered in depth in a chapter that Nino had found particularly interesting.

When class was over, and before he could move out of his seat, a hand extended into his line of sight.

"Hi. I'm Phyllis."

Nino took her hand and gently shook it as he turned to see her.

"Nino." He immediately began to sweat. There was nothing he could do to stop it.

"You Italian?"

"Yeah. Nino Lombardo."

"Phyllis Caruso. You're smart. We should study together. Do you want to get some coffee?"

Nino was struck. Not by Cupid's tiny arrow. This was love's version of the St. Valentine's massacre and he was a dead man. To his eyes she was a Neapolitan vision. Jet-black hair with matching eyes. A fabulous smile that shone in contrast to perfect olive skin. Her nose, well it was a little too big and like many Italian noses would be immense when she became an old lady. But for now, it was fine. Phyllis was petit. Tiny. One false move and he might crush her. Her beauty left him tongue-tied. She didn't wait for an answer.

"Come on. Let's go."

Phyllis got up and walked from the classroom. Nino, under her spell, followed.

She led him to Overfloweth, a beat scene coffee house situated down the block from The New School.

As they sipped espresso she filled him on the details. She was twenty-five, still living with her parents in Brooklyn. His old neighborhood. Not that far from his parents. She said she worked in the world of finance. She was a bank teller, a part time job that paid her way through undergraduate work and now through The New School's masters program. Her dream was to be a psychologist.

"So, what do you do, Nino?"

"I'm also in the world of finance. I make consumer loans." It was an explanation that Mickey conjured up so that Nino would have an acceptable answer to the frequently asked question. It satisfied Phyllis' curiosity.

"How come you're in Ivanofsky's class?" she asked.

"To tell you the truth, I don't really know. I just find it interesting."

"Do you want to study together tomorrow night? You can come to my parent's house."

He hoped she couldn't actually see his heart pounding under his shirt. "Yeah. Sure."

Nino walked Phyllis to the subway station. She once again shook his hand which retained just enough of her fragrance to get him back to his tiny Westside studio apartment. He spent a restless night unable to stop thinking about Phyllis Caruso.

The next morning Nino planned his day around a trip to Brooklyn. He would make his usual rounds in the morning, meet with Harry Moskowitz, a Jew with a seemingly endless supply of hot, high-end watches, go see his father about the thirty grand for Mickey, grab a quick bite for dinner, and then go study at Phyllis' house.

After his morning shower, he gave himself an extra squirt of deodorant under each arm. This would be a stressful day. Asking his father for Mickey's loan would normally be stressful enough. But just the thought of going to Phyllis' house was enough to get the sweat running.

The meeting with his father was surprisingly easy. Vito Lombardo was in the midst of putting out a fire when Nino arrived at the storefront clubhouse that served as headquarters for Lombardo's band of merry men. The Lombardos were part of the Genovese crime family. One of Vito's lieutenants had inadvertently wacked a member of the rival Bonanno crime family. It was a mistake. Mistakes happen. Vito was busy calling various members of the Bonanno family trying to convince them that an all out war between the families would only be bad for business and was completely unnecessary. Nino made his request between calls. His attention on other things, Vito approved Mickey's loan without doing his normal due diligence.

The visit to Phyllis' house wasn't as bad as he feared either. Phyllis was the eldest of eight. Her father, mother and seven brothers, from twenty-three-year old Francisco to two-year old Enrico "Ricky" Caruso were glued to the tiny black and white TV. Bruno Sammartino, an up and coming Italian-American wrestler was fighting at Madison Square Garden. The family hardly gave Nino a second look after exchanging pleasantries. Phyllis led Nino down to the finished basement so they could begin their studies. Knotty Pine paneling on the walls, a tiled floor, a couch, a record player, a card table, the basement was the domain of the Caruso children. Having a place to send the kids between meals was the only way to maintain sanity in a four bedroom house with 10 inhabitants. Phyllis and Nino would have the basement to themselves. They sat at the card table and began to study or what looked like studying. Nino although he was looking down at his textbook was desperately trying to think of something clever to say.

"This is a very nice card table," was the best he could do.

"You know I need to thank you."

"How come?"

"I was going to ask for a raise at the bank today when I saw my boss. But when he came in I was too scared to ask. Then I remembered what you said the first night you came to class. I noticed you right away. And then when Professor Ivanofsky asked you a question you just said, 'Sometimes you just gotta do what you just gotta do.' I really liked that. So at the bank I said that to myself. I said, "Phyllis you just gotta do what you just gotta do." And I asked for the raise and got it. So thank you."

"Yeah. No problem." Still not clever. He went back to his book.

They each tried their best to concentrate. But the room was rampant with pheromones. Phyllis got up and went to the record player. She put on a Frankie Avalon album. As Frankie began to sing *Venus* Phyllis retuned, not to the card table, but to the couch. She patted the cushion next to her indicating that clever or not, Nino should join her.

He sat next to her. She put her hand on his leg.

"You know what? I think I like you," she said.

He had nothing clever, unclever, nada. So Nino, mustering all the courage he could manage, leaned over and kissed her. It was the sweetest kiss either of them had ever experienced. It lingered. When they finally broke apart both their faces were the definition of joy.

"Look at you Mister Big Shot, kissing a girl without even asking her permission."

He laughed. "Hey, sometimes you just gotta do what you just gotta do." And he kissed her again.

SIXTEEN

Jimmy "The Artist" had the Columbia University transcript in an envelope and the forged sheep skin diploma already framed when Nino picked it up. The perfect replicas were well worth the two hundred dollars Nino insisted Jimmy take in return for his artistry. Carrying it down the street, Nino couldn't have been more proud had he actually gone to Columbia. He was in a great mood. And it wasn't just because of his newly printed faux academic bona fides. Nino Lombardo was in love. He would deliver the transcript and diploma to Ivanofsky, make a couple of collections, call Mickey at the office and make up some excuse as why he couldn't meet him for lunch, and then meet Phyllis. It would be the second day in a row that they would have lunch together. And today he would take her to Sclafani's.

Nino found Ivanofsky's fifth floor office, the one where he saw patients, in a nondescript midtown building on fifty-eighth street. On the door was stenciled, "Dr. Peter Ivanofsky, PhD." As he opened the door, a buzzer announced his arrival. The outer office was small with a love seat, two end tables with lamps and a small cocktail table with a few scattered magazines. The door to Ivanofsky's inner office was closed and Nino could hear the muffled sound of voices. He took a seat on the couch and approached a very difficult doctor's office decision: look at an old issue of National Geographic magazine which would certainly have pictures of bare breasts, or an old copy of The New Yorker which, even though he loved the cartoons, Nino only got to see in doctors' offices. He was in the middle of a mental game of eenie, meenie, minee, moe, when the door to Ivanofsky's inner office opened. Out came the good doctor accompanied by a young woman who had obviously been crying. Her nose was red. Her eyes swollen. She clutched a tear soaked tissue.

"I'll see you next week," Ivanofsky told her. "Believe me, just stop calling your boyfriend twenty times a day and things will get better."

That news made the woman burst into heavier sobs as she left.

"Come in, Nino. Come in."

They sat down in two comfortable chairs that faced each other. Nino unwrapped his diploma and held it up for Ivanofsky to see.

"That is beautiful work."

"Yeah, I know," Nino said. "It's a shame because who's going to see it?"

"Your patients. You will be seeing patients right away."

"Forget the patients. You're the one who's nuts. Just because I have a diploma? The people will know I'm full of shit."

"You have more than a diploma. You have two. I was able to get you also a New School diploma. It was not so difficult. Look I have already hung it."

There on the wall was a freshly hung New School diploma that read: "The New School for Social Research, in recognition of the satisfactory completion of study and upon the recognition of the faculty of The New School hereby confers upon Nino Lombardo the degree of Master of Arts." The President and the Dean signed it. To the casual observer, it looked very official.

"Once we hang the Columbia diploma, this is what your patients will see. Believe me they will not question you about this. And you are coming to class so you will learn things."

"How the fuck would I know what to do?" Nino protested.

"Nino, my friend, you have been given a gift. I noticed it the first time you came to my class."

"What are you talking about? What kind of gift?"

"You just gotta do what you just gotta do. It is perfect. Look, the hardest thing to do is to get people to change their behavior. They come to me for years before they change. You know this to be true, no?"

"Yeah. Look at you. Are you ever going to stop gambling even though I may beat you silly?"

"No chance. Exactly. But when you explain to people that they just have to do what they just have to do, and when you say it in your tone of voice, well this may actually get them to do what they have to do."

"Yeah but usually I'm also slapping them around when I'm saying that."

"No. This will arouse suspicion."

"If I see them without having a license, isn't that illegal?"

"I am assuming you will not have a problem with that. And by next week we'll have a phony license to hang as well. Look, I am aware that there are risks involved. But I am even more aware that I don't want you to beat crap out of me. I want this to work. I will share this office space with you. I will put your name on the door. I will refer clients to you. Only the mildly neurotic, like the woman who just left. These are women who want to know why men don't listen to them or why men can't be more like women. Things that will never happen no matter what you do. Most of them have to move on with their lives. They just need to do what they just need to do. Believe me, they will love you. You will sit with a pad on your lap as if you're taking notes, you will listen, try not to doze off, and if they turn out to be truly crazy, you send them back to me."

Nino looked around the office. He pictured himself sitting in the chair with a client lying on the leather couch. He would not be beating people up. He would be helping people. Maybe Ivanofsky was right about Nino's gift. After all, it had worked for Phyllis. He handed the Columbia diploma to Ivanofsky.

"Hang it up."

"Then you agree?"

Nino answered with a smile and a "I think I gotta."

SEVENTEEN

Tippy now knew three things: 1. she was not going to be the assistant to literary giant Norman Mailer, 2. she was not going to be a hotdog vendor, and 3. she was more determined than ever to get into the business world. The question was how? Mickey wasn't going to help her find the answer. Was there a business muse, a guide, or a mentor who could give her advice? As she racked her brain her thoughts were interrupted when the phone rang.

"Tippy, it's your mother," Barbara Vanhouten slurred having just returned from a four martini lunch. Without waiting for Tippy's response, Mrs. Vanhouten got down to business. "Doctor Collins tells me that he had to up your medication because you still don't want to get pregnant. Is that true?"

"Why is that old quack calling you? I'm his patient."

"Yes, but I'm paying him. And how dare you call him a quack. He's the top man in his field."

"Mother, you say that about every doctor you go to. 'He's the top man in his field.' Who told you that? Him? For all you know Collins might have barely gotten through medical school."

"All right, I'll give you that one. He doesn't seem that bright, does he?"

"Look, someday I may want a baby, but not now."

"My god, you're almost twenty-seven. In another six months your baby parts will begin to shrivel."

"In that case I'll have a baby this afternoon."

"If only you could. I don't like your attitude about this, Tippy. Why don't you to come home so we can talk about this? Come discuss this with your father and me."

Normally this would be the point where the argument would escalate and Tippy would end the call. Instead, what her mother said was an inspiration. Her father! Of course. He was the successful businessman in whom she needed to confide.

"Fine. I'll come up tomorrow and stay a few days. Have Toddy pick me up at noon," Tippy said.

"I can pick you up," Mrs. Vanhouten suggested.

"I don't care. Which ever of you is more sober."

"Look for Toddy."

~

That night at dinner Tippy told Mickey that she was going to be visiting her parents for a few days.

"You don't want me to come?" Mickey asked even though they both knew he didn't want to go.

"If you're there we can't tell Jew jokes."

He laughed and was relieved that he wouldn't be going. Mickey also immediately began planning how he might use the two days alone to end the relationship with Charlotte.

The next morning Tippy packed a small bag and took the train to Stamford. Each day thousands of people made the commute from Connecticut to Manhattan. It dawned on Tippy, while the train chugged out of Penn Station, that it would be just as easy to make the trip to Stamford every day if she was working for her father. Rolling along toward Connecticut, she began to think about fasteners. It's not something people think about very often. But Tippy had grown up around the family business. She loved the occasional Saturday when her father would take her to the factory. While he worked, she got to play in the storage area where millions of nuts and bolts awaited shipment around the world. If she got really lucky, Howell would take her onto the factory floor. The noise was so deafening it was enough to scare adults. Tippy was too fascinated to mind. She loved watching the giant machines pounding and pressing the thick steel wire into nails and screws. Pulling into Stamford station she searched for an idea that would bring new value to the family business. If she could come up with something new it might convince Howell to allow her to work for the family business.

Toddy was leaning against his new Chrysler 300 convertible, doing his best James Dean impression when Tippy got off the train. The car was his rich boy rebellion. The Brooks Brothers suit and rep tie that Howell demanded he wear made looking cool completely out of the question. Toddy was known as the family ne'er-do-well, flunking out of numerous private schools, out of college, flunking the army entry exam, as well as a number of roadside sobriety tests over the years. So when Tippy got in the car he couldn't wait to share his big news. "Dad has given me a promotion. I'm in charge of finding a new location for the factory."

"Why is he moving the factory?"

"We need more room. And he's put me in charge." Toddy bragged. "I'm looking at a property right after I drop you off at the country club. Mom wants to have lunch there."

Tippy was hardly paying attention. She was amazed to see how fast the town was growing since she had left. They passed a huge new store that she had never seen.

"Whoa. What is that?"

"Two Guys From Harrison. It's like a department store, only spread out instead of having lots of floors. It's an odd mix, they sell groceries, and clothes, and hardware."

"Pull in. Pull in. I want to see."

Toddy swung the big Chrysler into the parking lot. Tippy hopped out and headed for a new shopping experience.

The store was massive. There was nothing like it in New York City. A store like this would take up too much real estate. Here in suburbia there was always room to spread out. Tippy made a beeline for the hardware department. The tool selection was limited and every tool was hung neatly on pegboard. It all seemed very sterile. Tippy figured that this was not where serious builders shopped. These displays were meant for the inhabitants of new homes in new subdivisions. People who only needed a hammer to hang a picture or a screwdriver to tighten a cabinet handle. But where were the nails to hang the pictures? Where were the screws? What kind of hardware department didn't have screws? Tippy walked the hardware aisles until she found a salesperson hanging up pre-packaged sink stoppers.

"Excuse me, where are your nails and screws?"

"We don't really carry them. We don't have the room for all the bins of nails and screws we'd have to carry. I think you have to go to a lumber yard to get something like that."

"Thank you." Tippy then turned to Toddy. "Take me to the factory. I want to talk to Daddy."

"But what about Mom? She's waiting for you."

"You go to the club and have a drink with her. That's all she really wants. She just doesn't like to drink alone."

Neither did Toddy. She did not have to twist his arm. He would spend the afternoon with his mother. As for Tippy, she had her idea.

Tippy found her father on the factory floor, wearing a leather apron, helping a machinist repair one of the giant stamping units that turn steel wire into screws. This was when Howell Vanhouten was his happiest, with sleeves rolled up, doing man's work. The technology for manufacturing fasteners had not changed that much since the family started the business back in Revolutionary times. The steel wire was fed into the stamping machine where it was die cut to size, then pressed to form the screw head, then passed through the unit that cut the threads, then the screw would be dropped into a finishing bin. A final dip into a solution that would prevent the screw from rusting, and voila, screws. The process was repeated hundreds of times per minute. The wire diameter and the cutting dies would change depending on screw size. But essentially it was the same process whether you were making a screw, or a nail, or a rivet, or any one of the hundreds of fasteners the Vanhoutens turned out. With a profit margin of only fractions of a penny per screw, the Vanhoutens had to sell millions of them to maintain their lifestyle. Keeping the old machines running was a challenge and no one was better at it than Tippy's father. In spite of his old-money airs, in his heart, he was a grease monkey.

Before she presented her plan, Tippy waited until they were back in the quiet of Howell's office. She started with small talk to soften him up.

"I hear you're going to move the factory to a bigger space."

"Where'd you hear that?"

"From Toddy. He said you put him in charge of finding a new spot."

"That's just to keep him out of my hair. We're not moving. We're doing fine where we are. Now what's going on, Tippy? You didn't come up here to talk about Toddy's promotion."

"Daddy, I want to come work with you here in the factory."

Howell waited until he removed his apron and replaced his suit jacket before answering. This was going to require an executive, not a mechanic.

"Are you finally leaving Mickey?" he asked with just a hint of joy in his voice.

"No, I'm not leaving Mickey. I wish you would stop asking me that. I want a job. I'll come up here every day by train. I've got ideas, Daddy. Ideas that can help the business."

He was tempted to give her a quick, "no." But he was smart enough to hear her out.

"Have you been in that new Two Guys store?" she asked.

"Why would I want to go into a store like that? It's got no style what so ever."

"What it's got is a hardware section with no screws and nails. They can't deal with the inventory. Everything they carry is pre-packaged and hung on a rack. What if we packaged the screws, ten screws to a pack, and sold it for a dollar. Think how much we'd make on each screw."

"Who's going to pay that much for a screw?"

"The people who are buying screw drivers in a place like Two Guys. They don't want a big bag of screws or nails. They just want to do a little job. If we do this we'll be making at least ten times as much per screw. It's the future, Daddy."

"But we make hundreds of different sizes. It'll cost a fortune to package all of those."

"We don't package all of those. We just package the most popular sizes. People aren't going to hang a picture with a three-inch nail. We still make those and sell them to lumber yards where builders can find them. But all the people moving into all the houses that are being built in the suburbs, they're going to want ten screws or ten nails and that's it. They probably only want one or two and the rest will sit in a drawer. Who cares? We'll make more on those ten screws than on fifty of the ones we sell everywhere else."

He had to admit, the idea had some merit. Making impulsive decisions, however, was not the way he did business. This would take some contemplation.

"Let me think about it. We can talk about it some more at dinner tonight."

"I want a job, Daddy. We'll get to see each other every day. Wouldn't you like that?"

"I suppose. Come on. Let's go home." On the way, not able to help himself he added, "This would be a lot easier if you were leaving Mickey."

Tippy might have been more apt to accede to her father's wishes if she knew what Mickey was up to.

∽

The Huntington Hotel in Jersey City was not exactly what Charlotte had in mind when she said she wanted to go on vacation with Mickey. But that's where he took her after explaining that he didn't want to waste the opportunity for them to get away together. Yes, Jersey City was just across the Hudson, and one would be hard pressed to call it a romantic get away destination. But Mickey did a great sales job and made it sound like they were headed to the honeymoon suite at the Plaza.

Charlotte left work early so she could pack a few special things for their night together. Mickey met her at the Port Authority terminal and their romantic journey began on a bus to Jersey City.

Mickey seemed nervous when they had dinner in the hotel dining room. Charlotte assumed he was being distant because he was either worried they'd run into someone he knew, or, she hoped, he was anticipating some special surprise from her when they got back up to their room.

And a special surprise it was. Normally, only Charlotte put on some form of fantasy-wear. Mickey was only required to react appropriately to whatever outfit Charlotte wore. But on this night Charlotte had a costume for each of them. They would both be participating in the role-playing extravaganza she had planned for months. Charlotte explained that he would be the toga-clad Roman senator. She would be the scantily clad Nubian slave. He wondered how Nubian the pasty white Irish girl could be but said nothing rather than dampen her excitement.

"We're going to have an orgy," she purred. "But, you know, only with the two of us because...well there's only two of us." With that she slipped into the bathroom to get into costume. Mickey was to get into his toga while waiting for her entrance. Instead he sat on the single, straight-back chair in the far corner of the room.

Mickey wasn't exactly sure what a Nubian slave would wear to an orgy, but whatever it was, it was taking Charlotte a long time to get it on. When she finally did appear, he had to admit, she looked incredibly sexy. She wore a leather bra that was barely able to contain her. Below, a few dangling ancient coins hardly covered anything of importance.

"Where's your toga, Senator?" she asked in a cute baby doll voice.

"Charlotte, we have to talk."

She may not have been the brightest girl in the world but she had heard these words from other men before. Having a talk was not what she wanted to do, especially dressed the way she was.

"What is it now, Mickey?" she asked, the baby doll voice replaced by worn-out-New Yorker voice.

"I'm sorry. I can't do this any more."

"You can't do what? You can't have the best sex you've ever had in your life? You can't have a good time? You can't do what you know in your heart you want to do?"

"I love my wife."

"Why the hell did you bring me to Jersey City to tell me this?"

"I don't know what I was thinking."

Mickey knew exactly what he was thinking. If there was a scene with crying or shouting or throwing things, any kind of tantrum at all, it would happen in Jersey City. News did not travel from Jersey City to Manhattan. There was no interest what so ever in whatever happened in Jersey City. Jersey City was safe and only a bus ride away.

"If working together is too uncomfortable, I understand. You don't have to worry about giving notice or anything like that. I'm sorry, Charlotte. I really am."

Mickey wasn't sure what the appropriate next move was. Should he hug her before leaving? She was more than half naked. That would only lead to trouble. He didn't want to debate his decision. There was really only one thing to do; He left and took the next bus back to New York as a once-more faithful, monogamous married man.

∼

While Mickey was getting his life back in order, Tippy was at dinner with her family. The Vanhoutens were regulars at Bondini's Ristorante. Big meat and big booze was Bondini's recipe for success. Menus were unnecessary. Whiskey sours, shrimp cocktails, prime rib, and a scoop of pistachio ice cream with a cup of coffee would be dinner for each of the Vanhoutens each and every time they ate here. The only variation; Mrs. Vanhouten and Toddy would double up on the cocktails.

Dinner started with Howell extracting promises from everyone that they would all be voting for Richard Nixon. Mrs. Vanhouten made some brief small talk gossip about a neighbor's son who had been one of Toddy's classmates and had just been awarded a Fulbright Scholarship. Toddy had become numb to the never-ending emotional paper cuts to his self-esteem. His only reaction was ordering a third whiskey sour.

Tippy wasn't much of a drinker. Her cocktail loosened her up enough to ask Howell, "Well, Daddy, what did you think of my idea today?"

"Actually I liked you idea. I think it has merit."

"What idea is that?" Mrs. Vanhouten asked while fishing the maraschino cherry from her drink.

"Tippy has a wonderful idea for the business. She wants to come to work at the plant," Howell said.

Mrs. Vanhouten laughed and said, "Well that's not going to happen."

"Mother," was all Tippy could come up with in protest.

"You're having a baby. You're not going to work at the plant." Then turning to her husband she added, "And if she does, both your lives will be hell." Mrs. Vanhouten downed the rest of her drink in one gulp as an exclamation point.

"This isn't right, Daddy. You know I can do the job. Please."

Howell didn't need to make a Do It/Don't Do It list to make his decision. Mrs. Vanhouten was more than capable of making his life a living hell.

"Your mother is right. You should have a baby."

"Daddy."

"The answer is no. Now, please, let's just enjoy our dinner."

EIGHTEEN

It was, without a doubt, Janet Parker-Simpson's favorite thing in the world. Four times a year she got to fly to Paris to see the latest from the fashion world and spend Misters Bergdorf's and Goodman's money. In a week's time she'd spend hundreds of thousands of dollars on women's wear from the finest couturiers. Knowing she would spend that kind of money, the designers and manufacturers treated her like a queen. She would be wined and dinned at only the finest restaurants. It was treatment she could never afford on a buyer's salary. Especially a woman buyer who in no way made as much as her male counterparts. Still, the perks of the Paris trips made her ignore any inequalities. She was living the high life.

After a few days of personal shopping and recovering from jet lag, Janet's first real business stop in Paris was the showing of the Summer 1961 line at Maison d'Armand. Armand, one of the first designers to go with a single moniker was young, hip and a huge seller at Bergdorf's. The son of a French tailor, Armand Bouchet found that, even as a young boy, he had an overwhelming love of women's clothes. They fascinated him. Actually it was both the clothes and the women that kept his focus. And so at the young age of fifteen, with an already impressive portfolio of sketches in tow, he became one of the few heterosexual apprentices at Chanel. He was a quick study and rose through the ranks at the famous fashion house. He stayed for six years until a chance meeting at a party with financier Claude LeMonde led to the creation of Maison D'Armand. It was an instant success and in the six years since its creation had become an absolute must for buyers from around the world.

Janet Parker-Simpson had to be very careful not to spend her entire budget at Armand's show. Settling into her seat amongst the glamorous crowd which consisted of young European royalty, the very wealthy, and buyers from around the world, Janet Parker-Simpson got goose bumps as the lights suddenly went down and music began to play. It was show time and Armand was known for putting on runway shows with all the excitement and glitz the fashion world had to offer.

Backstage was a madhouse. Dressers, make-up artists, and hairstylists all worked at a million miles an hour getting the models ready for the show. In the middle of the mayhem, Armand was aware of every detail. Armand, tall, slim, with chiseled features and Caribbean blue eyes, he could easily be mistaken for a male model.

Debuting a new line in a new decade was both challenging and exciting. Armand, like many other young designers, was leading the cultural revolution. Hemlines were on the rise. Bold patterns and colors expanded the artist's palette. The old rules were ignored. There were no rules.

Armand checked out a stunning redhead, one last time. She looked fabulous.

"*Bon. Tres jolie.*"

"*Merci.*"

It was time to find out how well he had done. He sent the model out on the runway. He could hear the cheers and applause from the crowd.

While Armand inspected the next model, Claude LeMonde a small, nattily dressed man in his fifties, sauntered across the backstage area enjoying the sight of the most beautiful half-dressed women in Paris. He couldn't help himself from grabbing one's ass as she went by. She slapped his hand but he only laughed and blew her a kiss. He made his way to Armand.

"Armand, the show is fantastique! We will do very well."

"How is it out there?"

"Packed. The buyers from Bergdorf and Neiman-Marcus are here. We need those orders. Be sure to visit with both of them."

"I thought I was to worry about the fashion and you were to worry about the business."

"It's not what we want. It's what they want. And they want Armand."

As the show went on the excitement built for the entire audience.

Well for the entire audience except for Janet Parker-Simpson. While the other fashionistas stood and applauded each new dress, she sat in her seat completely confused.

During the finale, when all the models took one last trip down the runway followed by a triumphant appearance by Armand, he couldn't help but notice that the entire room was giving him a standing ovation except for one person in the front row - Janet Parker-Simpson.

As soon as the show ended, Armand made his way to her.

"*Bonjour*, Janet." He kissed her hand before adding, "Always good to see you."

"*Bonjour*, Armand. *Merci*."

"How did you like the show?"

"To be quite honest, I found it a little confusing."

"Confusing? *Pour quoi*? The hem lines are not that short."

"Armand, another designer showed me most of the dresses you showed tonight a few days ago in New York. I bought everything."

"Bastards!"

"You know who it is?"

"No. But I'm not surprised. A few weeks ago a set of sketches and designs were stolen. I wasn't that concerned because we've always had knock-off artists. But in the past they at least waited until we debut the line and make our sales. Now they are beating us to the market. This is no good. I want the name of the person who sold you these dresses."

"Gee, I feel funny turning him in."

"How will you feel when your customers find out you are selling counterfeit Armand?"

"Mickey Daniels. His name is Mickey Daniels."

∼

Mickey stood in the middle of Thirty-second Street watching Leroy and a truck driver unload huge rolls of fabric. They took each bolt from the truck and placed it on a handcart. When the truck driver got to the last piece of goods, he rolled it off the truck and on to the street.

Mickey hollered, "Hey be careful."

"That is careful." There is no intimidating New York truck drivers.

Mickey helped Leroy boost the huge roll on to the handcart and the two men pushed it on to the freight elevator. Before the door closed Nino arrived on the scene. He joined Mickey for the ride up to T&T Fashions.

"This is it?" Nino asked as he felt the goods.

"This is it," said Mickey. "Did you give your father the twenty grand?"

"Yeah. He said 'Good boy.' I think the last time he said that to me was when I beat up some kid in the eighth grade."

The elevator arrived at T&T. Mickey and Leroy pushed the handcart off of the elevator. Nino felt better actually seeing the goods arrive safely.

"Now that this seems to be going so good, Pop's gonna grab Armand's Fall line too," Nino said.

"Just like that? He knows he can get it?"

"It's an easy deal. Armand's brother is getting them. Do you believe that? His own brother."

Just as Mickey and Leroy got the goods to the cutting table, Charlotte stuck her head out of the office door.

Charlotte had returned to work the very next day after the trip to Jersey City as if nothing had happened. But, as she had explained to Mickey, she didn't want to lose her job just because of his change of heart. They were both adults and should be able to continue their work relationship. She was willing to accept his new boundaries and honor his decision. The only noticeable changes in her behavior; she was colder and more distant when dealing with Mickey, but at the same time she began wearing clothes that bordered on inappropriate. Plunging necklines and skirts slit up the leg would test Mickey's resolve on a daily basis.

"Mickey, there's a Barry O'Brien on the phone."

"Our boy from Bergdorf's is checking up," Mickey said to Nino. "Let's go give him the good news."

Mickey walked into his office and picked up the receiver.

"Barry, Mickey. How ya doin'?"

Mickey held the phone tightly to his ear. Nino could not hear O'Brien as he began his tirade.

"How am I doing? I just got a call from Paris. What did you do? You came in here with stolen goods."

Mickey would have to answer the question with Nino present.

"Stolen goods? No. I swear those dresses were made in my factory."

"You're full of shit. I may lose my job, asshole."

"Look, there's got to be a mistake. Let me see if I can straighten this out."

"You can't," O'Brien said. "We're canceling the order. Don't ever call me again."

With that Barry O'Brien hung up. Mickey gently put the receiver back on the cradle. He took a deep breath before looking Nino straight in the eye.

"Nino, I've got an idea. And I mean it, on this one there's no risk."

"No more ideas, Mick. We're done."

NINETEEN

It took another two days before Nino could muster the courage to just do what he knew he just had to do. He picked up Mickey at T&T Fashions and took him to Brooklyn.

Tony Carbellano had the look of a small time hood which, as it happened, was indeed his occupation. Dressed in a sharkskin suit, with a skinny black tie, Italian shoes so pointy that his toes ached all day, and hair so slick it looked as if it was lacquered. He leaned against a spotless 1960 Cadillac Fleetwood, a lit cigarette and a toothpick dangling from his lips. The car was parked in front of an unassuming middle class home in the Sheepshead Bay section of Brooklyn. He hardly moved a muscle when Nino and Mickey approached.

"Is Pop home?" Nino asked.

Tony answered with a nod. Nino and Mickey climbed the steep stairs to the row house. Nino found the front door unlocked. He and Mickey entered the dimly lit hallway. The house was oddly quiet. As they moved through the living room and on to the kitchen, Mickey couldn't help but notice that there was nothing to suggest that as Vito Lombardo's power increased, so did his taste. The house was decorated with so many tacky religious artifacts and bad reproductions of the works of Michelangelo that it was impossible to be anywhere in the house without Jesus looking at you. In the kitchen, there was a pot of sauce on the stove but no one around. Nino checked the sauce. It was still simmering. He gave it a stir.

"Hey, Pop? Ma?"

There was no answer. Nino did not like the looks of things. Where were his parents? His father had more than enough enemies. His mother would never leave a pot of sauce unattended. Nino put his finger to his lips telling Mickey to keep quiet and then drew his gun from his shoulder holster.

Mickey's heart pounded. This was not what he had bargained for. They headed down a hallway toward the back of the house. The old wood floors creaked with each step.

Suddenly one of the doors flew open. Nino leveled his gun. Out stepped sixty-year-old Vito Lombardo with his gun drawn and pointed right at Nino.

"Pop!"

"Nino."

Both men kept their guns at the ready. With his free hand, Vito reached behind himself and quickly closed the bedroom door.

"What are you doing?"

"I thought something happened to you and Ma."

"I thought someone was in the house."

It took a moment for the adrenalin to settle in both men before they put their guns down.

Mickey was surprised how unassuming Vito looked standing in the hallway dressed in just his boxer shorts and undershirt. Even though Vito was slightly built, Mickey always thought of him as bigger than life when dressed in his usual black suit. In fact, this was the first time in all the years he knew the Lombardo family that Mickey had seen Vito in anything but his very formal suit and tie.

"What are you doing here?" Vito asked.

"We need to talk." Nino said. Then noticing his father's attire he added, "You okay?"

"Uh, yeah. I'm just...uh...taking a nap before lunch. That's all. Come on."

Vito ushered the boys back toward the kitchen. Before they got there Marie Lombardo, Nino's fifty-eight-year-old mother came out of the bedroom. Marie was a big woman built very much like Nino. She wore one of Mickey's housecoats.

"Ma, you okay? Nobody's watching the sauce."

"Yeah, I was..."

"Watching me take a nap," Vito said.

"That's right. We thought you were going to call now before you visit," Marie said.

"I know. But it's hard to get used to not living here."

"Call."

"I know but I needed to see Pop."

"Call."

"How are you doing, Mrs. Lombardo? You like that housecoat I sent over. You look gorgeous in it," Mickey said.

"Yeah. Make sure Nino calls."

They entered the kitchen and Marie went to work on the sauce. The men sat at the kitchen table.

"So what gives?" Vito asked.

"You know those designs I sold?"

Vito looked at Mickey and said, "He did all right. He's a good boy."

"Yes he is."

"We got a problem." Nino said.

"A problem?"

"Yeah."

"Okay, there are ways to take care of problems."

Mickey did not want to know the ways. "Mrs. Lombardo really does look gorgeous in that housecoat. Doesn't she?"

"Actually, it's a little tight," Marie said. "It's chaffing me right under my arms."

"Well it looks gorgeous."

Vito wasn't about to be distracted. "Come on, Nino. What gives?"

Nino took a deep breath. "Okay, the guy I sold the plans to is the same guy I lent the thirty grand."

"Let me get this straight. You let him use our money to buy our plans?"

"Yeah."

"I don't like that," Vito said.

"Look, I trust this guy like a brother."

"Then what's the problem?"

"My brother can't pay."

"Can't pay?" Just the thought of getting stiffed had Vito clutching the bread knife that was lying on the table.

"No, Pop. The order he had for dresses got cancelled. He used some of the money to buy the goods to make the dresses. Now he can't pay."

"Did you...you know...convince him that he should do everything in his power to come up with the money?"

Mickey said, "The guy's good for the money. Like Nino said."

Vito turned to Nino. "Mickey knows your business?"

"He knows the guy."

"How many times have I told you not to do business with friends? 'The guy's like a brother.' Jesus H. Christ. What do we do?"

Marie said from the stove, "You gotta kill him."

"But he's like a brother," Mickey said.

"Hey, why have rules?" Marie said as she served them each a heaping plate of spaghetti with meatballs and sausage.

"I don't want to kill him," Nino said.

"I think you gotta. People find out I'm soft over thirty grand they'll take advantage. You better kill him," Vito said, taking a bite of pasta. "Marie, this is beautiful." Then, turning to Nino he said, "Yeah. Kill him."

"Your father's right. Kill him." Marie said while grating fresh parmesan over her husband's plate.

"Pop."

"What? Just do it. Now eat."

Mickey and Nino picked at their food while Vito and Marie dug in. After a moment, Mickey broke the silence.

"It's me, Mr. Lombardo. I'm the one who owes you money."

"You?"

"Yeah."

Vito asked Marie, "He's gonna kill Mickey?"

Marie answered with a look and shrug that said, "Why not?"

"I'll pay you back somehow. I just need a little extra time. And you got the twenty for the plans. It's only really ten thousand."

109

"But I don't think we can sell those plans now. I'm out that twenty. Mickey, you've always been like a son to me. But you took advantage of Nino. Now you're trying to take advantage of me." After a cold icy stare, Vito turned to Nino. "Did you give him the 'why guys like me don't do business with guys like you' speech?"

"Yeah, Pop. I did."

Vito began to twirl a mouthful of spaghetti onto his fork. "Mickey, I want fifteen grand in two weeks. Normally I'd say in a week but you're like family. Then I want the rest two weeks after. And since you're like family, I only want twenty percent interest."

"But that's impossible, Mr. Lombardo."

"Then Nino's going to kill you." Then turning to Nino he added, "And if you don't do it, I will."

With that, Vito and Marie resumed their assaults on their plates of pasta. Mickey and Nino sat speechless. Then Marie said, "Boys, eat while it's hot."

TWENTY

~~~~

Nino didn't head back to Manhattan with Mickey. Instead, he made a few collections in Brooklyn and then met Phyllis when she finished her day at the bank. He didn't want to think about the meeting with his parents and Mickey. The idea that he would have to treat Mickey like any other dead beat made him miserable. Time with Phyllis was light and easy. Time with Phyllis made him happy.

On the days when she didn't have to get to classes at The New School after work, Phyllis babysat with two-year-old Ricky. She would often take him down to the pier at Sheepshead Bay where Ricky would point out each and every "boat, boat, boat."

Nino and Phyllis, each holding one of Ricky's tiny hands walked slowly along the pier. Phyllis could tell that Nino's mind was a million miles away.

"What's going on, Nino?"

"It's nothing."

He wasn't talking. They kept walking. Halfway down the pier Ricky got tired. He lifted his arms to Nino to pick him up. Nino did.

"Nino," Ricky said and grabbed Nino's nose. Nino smiled and grabbed Ricky's nose.

They continued walking. Phyllis could see that holding Ricky had softened Nino's mood.

"Something happen at work today?"

He wanted to tell her the truth. His normal day was so filled with lies. People lied to him about when they would pay. He lied to them about what he would do if they didn't. But what truth could he dare say to her? I'm a loan sharking gangster who steals shit and beats people up. Oh, and I also love you.

"No. Nothing happened. Everything is fine." He shifted Ricky to one arm and put his other arm around Phyllis as they strolled down the pier.

∼

When Mickey got home Tippy had not yet returned from Connecticut. He sat at the kitchen table and opened a Dr. Brown's cream soda, his version of an evening cocktail. How on earth could he come up with fifteen thousand dollars in two weeks? There was no way. And even if there were a way, he would need another fifteen thousand soon after. Plus interest. Mickey was not one who was easily defeated. But here was a mountain that perhaps was too high to climb. Here was proof that the life he thought had been resurrected was now worse than it had ever been and that he was a fool of unfathomable proportions.

Tippy was in no mood to play the supportive wife when she came home. The trip to Connecticut was a failure. She had not gotten a job with her father. Her mother was unrelenting in her procreation campaign. The train ride home was filled with dread. She was returning to what? To a life without purpose? To a marriage that seemed to have lost its spark? That was confirmed when she walked into the apartment and Mickey didn't even bother to get up to greet her. There was no hello, no how was your trip, no good to have you home. What did Mickey come up with?

"Do you think your father could lend me fifteen thousand dollars?"

"Why don't you call and ask him?" She went to the bedroom to unpack.

They managed to agree on a restaurant for dinner. Other than that, little was said that night.

The next morning Tippy asked Mickey why he needed fifteen thousand dollars.

"Problems at work."

"I thought you had some new big deal."

"It didn't work out. Okay? It didn't work out."

He wasn't up for a fight. He got up and left for the office.

Mickey's morning commute to T&T Fashions was spent imagining the worst possible scenarios if unable to pay back the money he owed Vito Lombardo. He was fairly certain that Nino would not kill him. But Vito...that was another story. As he crossed the factory floor, Myron the old cutter called out to him.

"This is beautiful material, Mickey. You're going to be proud."

"Yeah. Make something pretty to bury me in."

Mickey entered the offices. Charlotte was at her desk. There was no, "Good morning," no wink, no smile, no evidence on her part that they had been lovers except that she was wearing an outfit that might make a stripper blush. Emotional winter had set in. Her outfit made him miss the heat of emotional summer.

"What's going on?" he asked.

"Nothing good: The Federal Trade Commission wants you at a hearing Monday morning to discuss whether they're going to close us down. Number two, we need to talk."

"About what?"

"About us."

"There is no us."

"That's why we need to talk."

"What else?"

"Actually I'm not sure if it's bad. There's a French guy in your office. And since he called you a lot of things in French that didn't sound very nice, I assumed it had to do with bad news."

"A French guy?"

"Yeah. Cute accent," she said.

"Okay. Give me a minute then come get me. Got it?"

"What will I say?"

"I don't know. Say I've got a big meeting."

"With who?"

"Come on, Charlotte."

"With whom?

Mickey entered his office and found the Frenchman sitting in his chair with his feet up on Mickey's desk.

"Why don't you make yourself at home?"

"This could be my home if I want. I could own everything you have."

"Believe me, all I have is problems."

"We'll see about that, Monsieur Daniels. My name is Armand. Does that ring a bell?"

"Well that's a great start to my day. You're the designer?"

"Yes. I design clothes. Clothes that look very much like the clothes being made out in your factory."

Just then, Charlotte opened the door and stuck her head in. "Excuse me, Mickey. It's time for your big meeting with...you know whom."

"Mr. Daniels is in his big meeting. Thank you," Armand said.

Charlotte looked to Mickey who gave her a nod to leave. She quickly closed the door.

"You are a very busy boy, Mr. Daniels. Stealing designs from me. Having an affair with your secretary."

"What are you talking about?"

"Oh please. I could tell the moment she walked in. Don't deny it. The French know these things."

Mickey took a seat across from Armand.

"So what do you want? You want my business? Take it. I can't do this anymore. I'm a dead man anyway. I owe the Mob thirty thousand dollars. The Federal Trade Commission is going to close me down. My wife is starting to suspect the affair. Which, by the way, is over. Who knows what you're going to do? You know, I wanted to be a big shot. Making robes and housecoats wasn't good enough for me. I wanted to be respected in the world of high fashion. That's a joke. No, I've had it. So whatever you want, Armand, it's yours."

"Mickey, may I call you Mickey?"

"What do I care?"

"Mickey, I want to solve all your problems."

"Yeah, right."

"I'm serious. I have a plan that I think will solve all your problems. You see I want to take you to France."

"No thank you. I'm sure the food is better but if I'm going to jail I'd rather do it here in the states."

"You are not the only one knocking off my designs. There are many thieves who are getting more and more sophisticated. So I want you to come to Paris and run my factory. I want to be able to put out my line with no lead-time. We will go into production at the last possible moment. Just the way you do here."

"And how is that going to solve my problems?"

"First, I will not have you arrested. Second, I will lend you the thirty thousand dollars you owe the Mob."

"Keep going." Mickey's interest was piqued. So far he liked what he was hearing. No jail. No murder. So far so good.

Armand picked up a few of the "Paris" labels from Mickey's desk. "As for the Federal Trade Commission, you won't be lying any longer. You will be making your clothes in Paris. And as for your wife and your mistress...you know having a wife and mistress; this situation is not so unusual in France. Once your wife and secretary are in Paris, maybe they'll accept the situation. You know, when in Rome..."

"Or in Paris," Mickey said.

"*Exactement*," Armand said.

"How would I explain it to my wife?" Mickey was having trouble putting all the pieces together.

"Tell her I've made you a wonderful offer. It's an adventure. Paris! The city of love. An opportunity to put the romance back in your marriage."

"I'd like that. And Charlotte? Wait a minute. Like I said, that's over. I wouldn't even have to take Charlotte. I could start fresh."

"That would be up to you."

"And I'd be making the kind of clothes I've always wanted to make."

"Legally, if you can stand it."

Mickey sat quietly for a moment going over the details. Was there a catch? Was he missing something?

"And the thirty thousand dollars, I get that now?"

"You get that once we start production in France. I need a guarantee that you'll deliver the goods."

"How about half? Can I get fifteen up front?"

"You know it's interesting, in both English and French the word for 'no' is 'no'. No?"

Mickey would still need a way to pay the thirty grand. Unless, of course, he could get out of the country before the first fifteen was due. That wouldn't make Nino happy but it would keep him alive. There was one last request.

"What about my factory? Some of these people have been working for my family for a long time," Mickey said.

"Well, well, I guess there is honor among thieves. Fine, you can keep knocking me off. Only now you'll do it at the appropriate time and we'll both profit from it. That is how you will pay back the money for the Mob."

Mickey and Armand spent the next few hours going over details. Mickey needed to get out of town fast. Who was making the reservations? Who was paying for the trip? Where would he and Tippy live once they got to Paris? Who was paying that rent? For whatever reason, Armand was very accommodating with all of it. He was willing to make all the arrangements.

"I don't get it," Mickey said. "This morning my life was shit. Now it's a bed of roses."

"Shit my friend is what makes the roses grow."

As Armand left Mickey's office, Charlotte walked in.

"What's with the French guy?" she asked.

Mickey took a moment before saying anything. He was still processing what had happened. "That was Armand, the big French designer. He's made me an offer. He's taking me with him to run his factory in Paris."

Without being asked, Charlotte sat down across from Mickey. "That's great. We'll have a wonderful time in Paris."

"What are you talking about? We're not going to Paris. I'm going to Paris. Charlotte, it's over."

"I don't think it is. Last night it hit me, why should I be the one who's miserable? I've decided that we're going to keep seeing each other."

"I can't do it."

"Sure you can."

"I can't. The cheating and lying are killing me. Do you understand?"

"I'll tell you what I understand. I understand that there's something special when we're in bed together. I know that and you know that. You can't deny it."

Mickey said nothing. He sat staring at the pencil he spun while looking for a new tack.

"Look, I've got to go to Paris and I need you here to run the factory," he said.

"Forget it."

"Forget it? This is a big promotion."

"Getting dumped is not a promotion. Is Tippy going?"

"What does that have to do with it?"

"If she's going, I'm going." Charlotte crossed her arms and legs to punctuate the point.

"Charlotte, somebody has to run the business in New York."

"Let Leroy do it. He knows more than you think. He'll be great at it."

"Charlotte..."

"Mickey, I'm thirty-two-year-old damaged goods. I've given away my prime years. Guys in New York are not lined up for girls like me. You're not leaving me and going to Paris. I'll do whatever I have to do."

"What's that supposed to mean?" he asked.

"It means either we continue seeing each other or else I tell Tippy about what we've been up to."

"You can't do that."

"Either I tell her or you tell her. But if we're not still together, she's finding out."

The thought of Tippy finding out was a punch in the gut. Mickey sat speechless. Charlotte got up and walked around the desk to Mickey. She bent over, once again giving him a clear view of the hypnotic serpent that lived between her breasts. She gave his inner thigh a squeeze.

"Don't worry sweetie, it's going be fine."

TWENTY-ONE

Nino was sweating bullets as he sat in Ivanofsky's office awaiting his first patient. The Russian had phoned Nino first thing in the morning and told him that he had an appointment at 10 am with a Martha Davenport. Ivanofsky was rushing to his morning class at Columbia and had time for only a few simple details about Miss Davenport, an aristocratic heiress wanting to go off the grid, psychologist-wise, because of the nature of her issue. Nino felt little reassurance when Ivanofsky's only advice was, "You're just gonna do what you just gotta do." Ivanofsky was laughing when he hung up.

The buzzer rang announcing her arrival. Nino took out his handkerchief, mopped his brow, and dried his hands best that he could before opening the door to the outer office.

Martha Davenport had the look of old money enjoying new times. The recent Sarah Lawrence grad wore a natural vicuna suit from Dior. Her hair was perfect, the result of a daily wash and set by Vidal Sassoon. Her tan recently freshened by a quick trip to her family's Caribbean compound.

Nino suspected she could afford to see whatever psychologist she wanted. Why would she want to see him?

"Thanks for seeing me on such short notice, Doctor Lombardo. Doctor Ivanofsky said he couldn't see me for a couple of weeks and that you were great."

Nino wasn't sure if he should correct her. After all, he wasn't Doctor Lombardo. He was Mister Lombardo. He only had a fake Master's degree, not a fake PhD. He let it slide and led her into the inner office.

She, luckily, knew more about the routine that he. She slipped off her shoes and lied right down on the leather couch. Nino grabbed a legal pad from the desk and sat in the adjacent chair. There was a moment of awkward silence since Nino really didn't know how the session was supposed to begin.

Finally he asked, "So, what's wrong with you?"

She sat up to challenge him. "What's wrong with me? There's nothing wrong with me. I have some issues that I'm working on. Wrong with me? Really?"

This was not the start that Nino was hoping for. He assumed if someone was seeing a psychologist there must be something wrong with them. According to Martha Davenport, evidently not.

"No. No. I didn't mean there's something wrong with you. Obviously if you're here there must be something bothering you. I should have asked what's bothering you, not what's wrong with you."

"Thank you."

"So what's wrong with you?"

"It's not me, it's my boyfriend."

Just as Ivanofsky had promised, he thought. "What's your boyfriend doing?" he asked.

"It's not what he's doing. It's what he wants me to do."

Nino's mind flashed on what he and his friends might have asked girls to do. Things the girls really didn't want to do like; keep the car running while I hold up this liquor store, or go pick up these hot watches for me because the cops won't be looking for you, or hide this money for me until I get out of jail. Those things all seemed pretty normal to Nino. He wondered what on earth could be bothering Martha?

"What's he want you to do?"

"He wants me to put his thingy in my mouth. Disgusting, right?"

Immediately Nino's face turned red and his thingy got hard. He shifted in his chair so the protrusion in his pants would not be so obvious. He covered it with the legal pad. Although Nino did not have a lot of experience in this department, he did have some. As a freshman at CCNY, Mickey had fixed him up with Janice Silverberg, a Jewish girl who, after a few dates that included extended make out sessions, explained that she would not "go all the way" because of Nino's Italian heritage. She would, however, be more than happy to put his thingy in her mouth. Nino loved having his thingy in Janice's mouth and dated her for several months until she got engaged to a nice Jewish boy. She never intimated that it was disgusting. In fact, she seemed to enjoy it. Nino considered relating the story to Martha Davenport but instead decided to go with his strength.

"You know, Martha, sometimes you just gotta do what you just gotta do."

"You mean I should just do it? That's not much help."

"I didn't say you should just do it. I said you just gotta do what you just gotta do. Look, some people don't find this kind of thing disgusting. That's their choice. Nothing wrong with that. You do find it disgusting. Okay, so what are you prepared to do? Have you told him you don't want to do this?"

"Many, many, many times."

"But he still asks?"

"Many, many, many times."

"Then maybe he's not the guy for you. And if he's not, then you just gotta do what you just gotta do."

"You mean break up with Nicky?"

"It's not always easy doin' what you know you gotta do. But if you don't, you wind up in a bad situation. You won't be happy. And I think that's what you want; to be happy. Am I right?"

"Well, of course."

"Then I think deep down you know what you've gotta do."

"I guess I better give that some thought."

"Yes, you should. Okay, what else you got?" Nino asked.

"That's all for today," Martha answered in confused tone. She expected the session to last longer.

"Great. Nice meeting you, Martha."

She wasn't sure what to do next. There was still plenty of time left on her hour. She stayed on the couch.

"Aren't we going to talk about why I get into these relationships and why guys always want me to do these kind of things?" she asked.

"Are you kidding me? Look at you. What do you think guys are going to want? If that's all that this Nicky wants then good riddance. But, if you care about each other, then you got to decide what's best for you. You just gotta do what you just gotta do. That's it."

Martha sat up. "Wow, Doctor Ivanofsky was right. You are very good. Thank you, Doctor Lombardo."

Once again, he did not correct her.

∽

Mickey had a very busy day. If he was really going to leave for Paris in three days there were a million details that had to be taken care of. He had to decide if Leroy was actually capable of keeping things running at the factory while he was gone. He had to track down Armand and tell him that travel arrangements for Charlotte had to be made. And he had to convince Tippy that, without much notice, they would be leaving for Paris.

When he got home Mickey found Tippy sitting at the dinette table having a cup of tea. The table had newspaper classified ads strewn all over it. A number of the ads had been circled.

"What's all this?" Mickey asked.

"I'm looking for a job."

"Jesus, Tippy, we've been over this. You don't need a job. You're not thinking clearly."

"Don't tell me what I need, Mickey. I'm getting a job. And for your information I'm thinking more clearly than I have in months."

"But I thought you wanted to have a baby. That's why you've been taking those pills."

"Everybody else wanted me taking those pills. And just so you know, I've also been taking pills so that I won't have a baby."

"You what?"

"I've been taking birth control pills so I won't get pregnant. Maybe someday we'll have a baby. But not now. Now I want to go to work. I want to feel like I have a purpose. And I'm to the point where I don't care what it is. Whether it's selling hotdogs or one of these jobs in the paper working as a secretary, it doesn't matter. And there's nothing you can say that's going to change my mind."

"Would it change your mind if I said we were moving to Paris?" Mickey asked with a sly smile.

"What the hell are you talking about? We're not moving to Paris."

"Actually we are. In a couple of days. The deal that I said fell through, well now there's a better deal. I've been offered the chance to run the factory of a big Paris designer, Armand. It's a chance to really learn the fashion business."

"And I'm supposed to just pack up everything and move to Paris? And why in a couple of days?"

"I know it's a little abrupt. But it's important that we get out of town…you know…leave right away." Mickey did his best to make their quick exit sound in some way sane.

"There's no way we can be ready to go in a couple of days. We have to get plane tickets…"

"Armand is taking care of it."

"A place to live…"

"Armand is taking care of it."

"Passports?"

"We'll have them tomorrow."

"Legal passports?"

"He's got connections. Think about it, Tip, Paris. And it's not just for work. I thought it would be a chance for us to get things going in the right direction again. Pairs. City of romance. We'll get away from all the distractions here. We'll be together. You'd like that, wouldn't you?"

She thought for a moment before answering. "I would like that," she said.

"Then come on. It'll be great. And you can sell hot dogs in Paris if you want to."

"You mean it?"

"Actually I don't know if they even allow hotdogs in Paris. Hotdogs may be against the law in France. I'm telling you, Tippy, it's going to be great. I promise."

"I don't know. Maybe I should call my father and see what he thinks."

"No. We can't tell anybody. Armand wants this to be top secret."

"Doesn't that sound fishy?"

"People are knocking off his line. He wants me to run production at the last minute so his designs aren't floating around where people can steal them. It's not fishy at all."

"But don't people need to know where we are? Did you tell Nino?"

"Not Nino, not anybody."

"The people at the factory must know."

"Leroy is in charge until we get back. He knows we're going away but he doesn't know where."

"You're putting Leroy in charge instead of Charlotte?"

"Charlotte is coming to Paris. She knows how the whole system works if I'm out of the office."

It all sounded crazy but at the same time plausible. The idea of getting her marriage back on track certainly sounded appealing. And there was no doubt that doing it in Paris sounded romantic. "Well, I guess. What the hell? Okay. Let's do it."

TWENTY-TWO

Rue du Faubourg Saint-Honoré had been the home of French high fashion since the 1800's. Lined with names such as Hermes and Lanvin, 23 Rue du Faubourg Saint-Honoré was the home of Maison D'Armand.

On the second floor, in an office bathed in natural light, Armand sat doodling at his drafting table, searching for an idea. He had spent the previous few days running around Paris finding an apartment for Mickey and Tippy and a studio apartment for Charlotte. He made sure the buildings were close enough to each other that Mickey could get from one to the other without wasting travel time. He assumed, in spite of Mickey's protestations that the affair was over, that if Charlotte was coming to Paris, Mickey would be a busy, busy boy. Armand wanted to be sure that Mickey would have enough energy left to keep to the breakneck production schedule that was soon arriving.

Armand roughed out a drawing that was more of an exercise to get his juices flowing rather than a serious attempt at design. There was a nervousness about him as his pencil moved around the sketchpad. He hoped it was the nervousness that often accompanied the creative process. He always felt uncomfortable just before inspiration would flow. This discomfort, however, felt different. There was more of a sense of fear rather than anticipation.

Armand's concentration was interrupted when Claude LeMonde entered.

"Armand, the production people are getting nervous. They need to get started on the Fall line and we haven't even seen sketches."

"If you keep bothering me I can't get them done."

"And how are we to make the Fall show?"

"This is my plan," Armand said. "I design the dresses at the last possible minute. That way the knock off artists have nothing to knock off."

LeMonde gave the idea some thought as he lit a Galoises. "I don't like it. I want to see something. Let me look."

"Fine. Look." Armand held up the sketch that even he, if pressed for an honest opinion, would have to admit was not up to his standards.

"It's hideous." LeMonde was not shy about criticizing Armand. After all, it was his money that helped build the empire.

"Of course it's hideous. It's not done yet. You don't understand the process. Do you think I just pull these things out of my ass?"

"This one, yes."

"Get out. Out! I will show you something when I'm ready."

Armand got up and led Claude LeMonde out of his office. As he walked back to his drafting table he heard the door open again. He turned, prepared to continue his argument with LeMonde. Instead he saw his brother, Henri.

Henri Bouchet was not nearly as dashing as his younger brother Armand. Where as Armand's skin looked healthy and robust, Henri's was pasty white. Armand had flowing curls, Henri a wild head of steel wool. Armand had the perfect Gaelic nose. Henri's thick glasses were perched on a nose the size of a petit baguette. Neither man particularly looked like their father which raised real questions about mom's *fidelité*

"And what do you want?" Armand asked.

"I want to surprise my brother and take him to lunch."

The offer disarmed Armand. He immediately went to Henri, embraced him, and exchanged brotherly kisses to each cheek.

"*Vin?*" Armand asked.

"*Certainment.*"

Armand opened a bottle of Chateau Margaux '53. He poured each a glass of wine. He then sat down at his drafting table. Henri moved behind him to see what he was drawing.

"How's it going?" Henri asked.

"You don't know what it's like around here. I wish we could trade places. How I envy you and your simple life as a cheese merchant."

"You mean instead of being surrounded by beautiful models, you would rather be like me and smell like cheese all the time?"

"You smell like the very best brie, Henri."

"Thank God for that. So how is the new line coming?"

Armand stared at his wine as he gave it a swirl. He took a sip before answering. "If I confide in you, Henri, you must swear that you will share this with no one else."

"You know you can trust me."

Armand held his glass up to the light and admired the deep red. He took another sip before admitting, "The new line isn't coming."

"There are no new drawings?"

"I don't know what to do, Henri. You are the only one I can tell of this. In my mind there is nothing. *Rien*. All my ideas are gone."

"You should not even joke like that, Armand."

"This is no joke. The place in my mind where the ideas are born... my muse...she's gone."

"What are you going to do?"

"I don't know. But I have brought an American to Paris. He has been using the plans which were stolen from me to knock off my line. He knows how to produce a line very quickly. I'm hoping Madam Inspiration will pay me a visit in time and I will make my deadline."

The brothers sat quietly for a moment sipping their wine, considering the dilemma.

"There must be a logical explanation. We must get your muse back. I leave for the United States in two weeks and I don't want to be worrying about you. I want to see all the new sketches for the new line before I leave."

"I hope I can. I don't understand what happened."

"Okay, when I make cheese it is very important that I follow the same steps time after time. Are you doing something different than usual when you design a line? Have you changed your diet?"

"No."

"Your tennis game?"

"Twice a week. Like always."

"Something must be different. You love life?"

"What love life?" Armand asked with a laugh.

"You are no longer seeing Isabelle?"

"No. *C'est fini.* She's decided she only wants to sleep with her husband."

"Why?"

"Women. Who knows? I miss our secret rendezvous. Do you know how exciting it is taking something that you know belongs to another man?"

"No. Why would I know that? No. Absolutely not. No."

"Okay, I believe you. You know, maybe it was Isabelle. Maybe she was my muse. I haven't had a new idea since she left. Maybe without her I'm nothing."

"Don't say that. It might not have been Isabelle. It could be that all you need is the excitement of an illicit affair. Maybe that's what gets your creative juices flowing. Maybe you just need to be sleeping with another man's wife. What do you think?"

"I guess if I had to," Armand said with a smile.

"You have to."

Henri offered his glass up in a toast.

"To your new affair."

"To my new affair."

Armand could only hope that this would truly be the solution to his problem.

∼

Tippy was unable to relax during their first week in Paris. The idea of telling absolutely no one about their adventure was stressful. She worried about her parents and what they would think when they were unable to reach her. Friends, neighbors, doctors, what would people do when someone they knew seemed to disappear from the face of the earth?

Tippy wrestled with the overstuffed chair thinking it might look better at the other end of her new living room. Armand, as promised, had made all the arrangements so that when Mickey and Tippy arrived in Paris they were able to go directly to their new apartment. He did a fine job. The cozy, furnished flat on Rue Ampere featured hardwood floors that made moving furniture in stocking feet almost impossible. When Mickey came out of the bedroom she was hoping for help.

"Mick, do you think this will look better over there?"

"Yeah. Sure. It'll be great."

"Do you want to give me a hand?"

"Absolutely." Mickey was doing all he could to be helpful. They had slept away their first day in Paris, suffering the effects of jet lag. The next few days were spent exploring the neighborhood and adjusting their circadian rhythms. Then it was time for Mickey to go to work. When he did, Tippy spent her days making their new home feel more like it was their home. And up until now Mickey was cooperating as much as possible. He wanted Tippy to feel settled. He wanted her to be happy. He wanted to raise as little suspicion as possible when he left to go to Charlotte's new apartment. She too was now in Paris and also wanted to be welcomed into her new home.

After helping Tippy move the chair, Mickey announced, "Listen, honey, I need to go for a little walk."

"You want company?" she asked.

"Not tonight, Tip. I need to clear my mind."

Tippy watched as Mickey put on his coat. "You know, when we decided to come to Paris I thought it was to change things, like you taking these walks alone."

"I just need a little time to figure out some things about work. Like how I'm going to get this line produced when this guy hasn't even gotten any sketches done. We'll get to see Paris together. I promise. How about lunch tomorrow? Okay?"

"I guess."

"There's not much for me to do until Armand starts designing. You'll come to the office and we'll spend the afternoon together. How's that sound?"

"That sounds good."

"I'll be back before you know it."

Mickey gave Tippy a quick kiss on the cheek. She plopped down into the chair and watched him go.

∼

Only a few blocks away, Charlotte entered her apartment building carrying bags of groceries. As she struggled with the bags while searching for her key, a tall, good-looking man came down the hall and went to the apartment across from Charlotte's.

"Can I help you with those Mademoiselle?" He didn't wait for an answer. He took the groceries from her.

"Thanks."

"Are you the new tenant from America?" he asked. She was relieved he spoke English. She had been trying to learn as much French as possible since she left New York. The day had been spent however, not being able to understand much of anything anyone had said to her.

"Uh huh...yes...oui."

"Ah, you speak French."

"I'm trying."

"*Bon soir*. My name is Paul. I live right across the hall."

"Charlotte. Nice meeting you." She extended her hand to shake his. Paul managed to reach out from the packages. With a hand that was black from grease.

"*Pardon*. I am an auto mechanic. Not really. I just do it for the money."

"What do you really do?"

"I make fuck music. You will probably hear me from my apartment. I hope it doesn't bother you. Do you like fuck music?"

Charlotte blushed. "I'm not sure I know what that is."

"In American you have Peter, Paul, and Marie. Pete Seeger. Very famous fuck singers."

"Folk singers! Yes!"

"You like?"

"Yes. I like."

"Good."

Charlotte got the door open and took the grocery bags from Paul. They stood quietly for a moment.

"Well I have to get dinner going," she said.

"Yes. Nice meeting you." Paul started toward his apartment then turned back to Charlotte. "You know maybe one day we should have lunch or something. I could show you Paris."

Charlotte immediately checked Paul's left hand for a wedding ring. It had been so long since she had been out with a single guy.

"Well...maybe...no. I don't think so."

"I heard 'maybe' first. How about tomorrow?"

How could she go? What would she tell Mickey? After making such a big deal of coming with him to Paris and now she'd be going on date before she was completely unpacked. Charlotte found it interesting that she was at all conflicted. Yes she had feelings for Mickey but she definitely found this Frenchman interesting.

"It's hard for me to get away for lunch sometimes."

"I see. Then perhaps some evening just for fun we can make fuck music together."

Charlotte immediately said, "No." Although she did think about what kind of costume she might wear if she was actually making fuck music. Perhaps something with a John Phillip Sousa theme. That should get everybody humping.

"Then have lunch with me tomorrow. Get to know your neighbors," Paul suggested.

"Well I guess there wouldn't be any harm in lunch."

"Great. *A demain.*"

Charlotte looked confused.

"Until tomorrow," Paul said.

"A demain," Charlotte said then entered her apartment.

The apartment was a small nicely furnished studio. She had hoped that her apartment in Paris would be bigger than her digs in New York. It was not.

Charlotte had just put the groceries down on the tiny dinette table when there was a knock on the door. It only took a few steps to get back to the door. She opened it and found Mickey, slightly out of breath, and not looking happy. She assumed he'd had a bad day. She could fix that. In reality he had spent the trip from his apartment to hers wondering what he was doing falling into the same trap that had held him hostage back in The States. What if he told Tippy the truth? That would disarm Charlotte. Then he would just have to convince Tippy not to leave him. That would require a hell of a sales job. He wondered if Nino would be willing to "take care" of Charlotte. There were two problems with that idea: Nino would know where Mickey was and would more likely "take care" of him rather than Charlotte. And even though Charlotte was making his life miserable, he wasn't prepared to have another human being murdered. At least he was pretty sure that was the case.

And as Tippy had pointed out, being in Paris was supposed to be different. The pangs of conscious had Mickey in a fairly foul mood by the time he reached Charlotte's apartment.

"Sorry I'm late getting dinner started. But wait until you see the cute little undies I found today."

Mickey walked in and began to get undressed. "No dinner, tonight. We don't have much time. I need to get home."

"Don't we have time for a glass of wine or something?"

"Not tonight."

They both undressed and fell on top of her bed. Without much foreplay, Mickey began to mechanically hump away. Charlotte felt numb as she stared at the ceiling. Then, as Mickey went about his business, she heard Paul's voice singing:

IF I HAD A HAMMER, I'D HAMMER IN THE MORNING.
I'D HAMMER IN THE EVENING. ALL OVER THIS LAND.

TWENTY-THREE

Nino was about to dial Mickey's number again when the office buzzer rang. He had been trying to reach Mickey for the past three days. But each time he called he got Leroy on the phone claiming that Mickey was out and that Leroy would give him the message. Mickey's first payment would be due in a few days and Nino wanted to be sure there weren't going to be any problems. In addition, Nino couldn't remember the last time Mickey and he hadn't talked to each other for more than a day. He wondered where Mickey might have gone and why he hadn't heard from him.

Martha Davenport was back even though it had been only about a week since her first appointment with Nino. She insisted on getting in to see him as soon as possible. Once again she walked into the office, kicked off her shoes, and got comfortable on the couch. Nino put took a pad from the desk and sat in the therapist's chair.

Having already gone through a session with her and feeling a bit more comfortable in his role as therapist, Nino started right in.

"What's wrong with you today, Martha?"

She gave him a most disapproving look.

"What? Do you want me to help you or not? It's your dime," he said.

Actually, she didn't mind his confrontational approach. "Well I thought a lot about what you said the last time and realized that I love Nicky. Plus he's from a very good family so I don't want to lose him. So I just did what I had to do and went ahead and put his thingy in my mouth."

"And?"

"Not as bad as I thought and the next day he went to Cartier and bought me a bracelet."

"I think the important thing is that you realized that you love him," Nino said. It seemed like a sensible thing to say. He thought that perhaps this was the key to being a psychologist; just give some common sense advice.

"Right. Plus it's a really, really nice bracelet. He's got taste. That's important too," she said while dangling her wrist in the air to show off her new bauble.

Nino thought to himself, the guy should have bought the bracelet a long time ago. It would have made getting the blowjob a lot easier.

"So what are you doing here today if we fixed everything?" Nino asked.

"Well now Nicky says he wants to put his head, you know, down there and kind of do the same thing to me. Disgusting, right?"

Nino did not answer right away. He sat rubbing his eyes wondering why this woman was coming to him for advice in this department. Finally he said, "You know what I think, Martha?"

"That I just gotta do what I just gotta do? I'm not sure that's going to help me with this."

"I think this is something that you should be talking about with your girlfriends. Do you have any girlfriends, Martha?"

"Yeah, but I don't think I can talk to them about something like this. They're all such gossips. It's much easier sneaking up here to talk to you, a professional."

"Times are changing, though. I don't think you're going to shock any of your friends if you ask about this."

"I'd be worried about what they're going to think of me," she said.

"You should be worried about what you're going to think if you ask one of your friends if this is disgusting and she says it's wonderful. What if she says she won't go to bed with a guy unless he does do this? What if she says no one is getting in the door unless they stick their head in and yell, 'is anybody home?' You know what I mean? Then what are you going to do?"

"I don't know. I'm supposed to be a good Catholic girl. I guess I'm afraid," Martha whispered.

"Of what?"

"Of all the Hail Marys I'm going to have to say. As it is all the stuff I'm doing with Nicky, when I go to confession, the Hail Marys they're taking up a lot of my time. Don't you think this is a sin?"

Nino wasn't sure how to answer. He had stopped going to confession long ago. He figured Jesus might have forgiven him the first few times he confessed to beating people up. But even He would get tired of hearing the same thing week after week. At some point Nino figured he was on his own in the sin department. Martha was waiting for an answer.

"That's a tough one, Martha. See it doesn't matter if I think it's a sin. It's if you think it's a sin. To tell you the truth, now a days I only go to church to keep my mother happy. But enough of that stuff has been pounded into my brain that I know when I'm doing things that I shouldn't do. Then there's the stuff that they tell you that you should feel guilty about that I don't think that Jesus cares about one way or the other. So personally, I think that if two people love each other and they're doing things that they both like and it makes them both happy, I don't think Jesus has a beef with that. That's what I think. But this is one you're going to have to figure out on your own."

"So I should try it first and then decide?"

"That's what I would do," he said matter-of-factly.

"Wow. You really are amazing, Doctor Lombardo."

"You can call me Nino." Being called "Doctor Lombardo" was a sin with which he had not yet made peace.

Martha wrote a check for thirty dollars, the fee Nino was charging for a session. She also made an appointment for the following week.

"And I'm going to send you some referrals. I have quite a few a girlfriends who should see you too, Doctor Lombardo..."

"Nino."

"Doctor Nino. It seems like everybody today has things that are confusing and you've got answers. Thank you so much."

Nino liked the fact that he had helped Martha. It felt good. Much better than the way he felt after terrorizing his usual clientele.

Once Martha was out of the office Nino sat looking at the check.

This was easy money. In some ways this seemed like more of a racket than his actual racket. He wondered what it would be like to be a full time psychologist. It would certainly be safer. He wouldn't have to lie about what he did for a living except for the fact that his credentials were counterfeit. The down side would be that it would be hard to make as much money as he was already making. Nino was pulling in about thirty-five thousand dollars a year. That was partly because he was the boss' son. To make that, though, he had to work long, unpredictable hours. Hijacking trucks and calling on deadbeats was not a nine to five proposition. It would take an awful lot of clients like Martha to make that kind of money. He wished he could find a way to work it out. He promised himself that he would. Nino took a quick look at his watch. Still running. He had a number of stops to make. This was going to be a busy day. He wanted to get done early so he wouldn't be late for dinner with Phyllis.

Leroy was sitting at Mickey's desk, going over the production schedule, when Nino arrived. Mickey and Nino spent so much time together that practically everyone at T&T Fashions knew Nino. No introductions were necessary.

"Leroy, where's Mickey?"

"Don't know, Nino."

"What do you mean, you don't know?"

"Mickey said I don't need to know where he is. He just said that I'm running the factory until he gets back."

"What about Charlotte?"

"She's gone to where ever too." Then, lowering his voice to a whisper, Leroy said, "It's none of my bees wax, but I think there may be some hoochie coochie going on between those two. If you know what I mean."

Nino walked over to the desk and stood over Leroy. He put his hand on the shipping clerk's shoulder and gave it a squeeze. "You've got two seconds to tell me where is he, Leroy."

"Hey, Man, be cool. I am not any kind of hero. If I knew I would tell you. All I know is that first we were making that line for Bergdorf's, the one that you knew about, and then we weren't. Then some French guy shows up and Mickey tells me that I'm making twenty bucks more a week, that I'm running the place until he gets back, that Charlotte has to go with him, and that he's not telling me where they're going."

"That's it?"

"Well he did also say that you would probably come here to beat the shit out of me but I should tell you that he knew that and that's why I couldn't know where he was going to be. So I think we've got to honor his foresight on this one and not bother with the beating."

"Son of a bitch."

"Can't argue with that one."

"You're sure it was a French guy?"

"Based on my high school French, *Oui*."

Nino went to lunch at his favorite burger joint on 34th. They made a great cheeseburger and he loved the way the burger was delivered to each counter stool by a Lionel train. Plus, no one there owed him money so he could be alone and do some serious thinking. He figured that Mickey had skipped town. Rather than admit that he failed to keep on eye on his friend, he decided that he would not rest until he found Mickey. Then he would either get the money or, yes, take care of things to the satisfaction of his father. Leroy said the guy in the office was French. Nino figured that it must have been the brother, Henri, the guy he met at the airport when he got the plans. He would check with this father and see how Vito originally contacted Henri. He had a hunch that contacting the brother would probably lead him to Mickey. While enjoying a slice of hot apple pie, another specialty of the house, he made one other decision. Taking care of Mickey would be his final criminal act. Life as a thug was not making him happy. He wanted a more normal life. He wanted a life with Phyllis. He wanted a life with no more lies...well except for the fake credentials. It would take years of study to put that lie to bed. But eventually, with some effort, that too could be made right.

Nino's next stop was at the Sherry-Netherlands Hotel where oil magnate Edgar Keeling was patiently waiting for his weekly rough-up. Nino didn't bother with his usual knock on the already opened door. He walked right in. Edgar took the opening line from their weekly performance.

"Nino, I'm sorry, I don't have this week's payment."

"Yeah, yeah. Don't worry, we'll get to the beating. But first I've got a question." Nino sat on the couch with Keeling. "Edgar, I've got this other client, a stock broker. He can't pay back his loan and, unlike you, he doesn't want me to slap him around."

"I don't either. I just don't have the money."

"Would you just wait a minute with that? I told you, we'll get to it."

"Fine. What's your question?" Keeling asked.

"Instead of paying me back, he wants to give me stock. Polaroid. He says in the next couple of years it's going to be worth a fortune and he says it pays dividends. You know, every few months they send him a check. He says the dividends will cover his loan and if things go good I'll make a bundle on the stock. You're a smart business guy. Does that sound right to you?"

"Obviously there's some risk. If the stock goes down you won't get as much. But yes, it's plausible. I actually live off the dividends from all the stock I own in my oil company." Edgar said. Then, realizing that bit of information didn't fit in with his tale of insolvency, he added, "But I still don't have today's payment."

"I'm warning you, if you say that again I'm not going to lay a hand on you. Is that what you want?"

Nino sat quietly for a moment. His mind was churning. Then he asked, "So if I wanted to make around thirty-five grand a year, how many shares of your stock would it take?"

"Well over the past few years we've paid a dividend of around a dollar a share. That's quarterly. So between eight and nine thousand shares would do it."

"Okay, here's what's going to happen, Edgar. I'm getting ready to retire. I'm getting out of the loan sharking business."

"Nino, no. You're so good at it."

"Just wait a minute. Who ever my old man sends over here to collect from you isn't going to want to play these games of yours. They don't' have time for the bullshit that I put up with. If you don't pay and they see how much money you really do have, they're gonna rob you, then they're gonna kill you. We don't want that, do we?"

"No. Of course not."

"Okay, so you're going to give me ten thousands shares of stock in your company and you're going to be the only loan that I still collect on. I'll come up here every Thursday, and you'll pay me."

"If I have the money. I don't today."

"Now I really am going to slap you. Listen, we'll do this for as long as you want. If you decide you want to pay off the loan, you'll pay and we're done. I keep the stock and we both live happily ever after. If you don't want to do it, next week Teddy No Nose will be here and he'll fucking kill you. So what do you think?"

"I think it's a marvelous plan. You'll have your Polaroid stock and my stock...It's good to be diversified. And you'll have a portfolio."

"I like the sound of that," Nino said.

"We can have my broker take care of the transfer of shares tomorrow." Keeling extended his hand to Nino to seal the deal. They shook on it.

"Is there anything else?" Keeling asked.

"Yeah. I want today's payment."

"I'm afraid I don't have it. I swear I don't."

Nino smiled, got up, grabbed Keeling by the lapels and pulled him to his feet. He slapped him twice and punched him in the stomach, doubling him over. Keeling fell to the floor. Nino walked to the desk and took the envelope with the money from the top drawer.

"I'll be here tomorrow morning so we can take care of the stock," Nino said as he headed for the door.

"Good to see you, Nino," Keeling groaned from the fetal position.

Nino wanted dinner with Phyllis to be special so he called Joey Sclafani and made a reservation. Joey promised him one of the booths that provided the kind of privacy you'd want if you were planning a heist, or a hit, or in Nino's case, just a nice quiet dinner. The fact that Nino called for a reservation alerted Joey that the evening would call for the ultimate amount of fawning. He would make sure that Nino and Phyllis had a night to remember.

That night, seated at the candlelit table, Phyllis looked beautiful. Nino sat across from her and took her hands in his.

"Phyllis, we gotta talk," he said.

"I don't like the sound of that. What did you do something?" she said with a smile.

"Yeah. I did do something. I've been lying to you about who I am."

"Really? Who are you?" she asked, no longer smiling.

"When I told you I was in finance, the truth is I'm a loan shark. I'm a gangster. A thug. I'm not a nice guy. But I decided today that I'm not doing this anymore. I've got a few loose ends to tie up but then, I swear, I'm done. I didn't tell you sooner because I figured if you knew the truth you wouldn't have anything to do with me."

"You think I didn't know? You're Nino Lombardo, son of Vito Lombardo. We both live in Brooklyn. Everybody knows who you are. Okay, you said you were in finance and you sort of were. We'll count that as an honest mistake. But you promise you're not doing it anymore."

"Like I said, a few loose ends, and that's it. I swear."

"Then I'm okay with that. What else you got?"

Nino sat quietly for a moment. In some ways this one was harder than the first. He took a deep breath and said, "I got fake credentials from Ivanofsky and I'm already seeing clients. But I want to go back to school for real and get legit. That's going to take a while so I'm thinking I'm going to use the fakes for the time being."

"Okay with that."

"All right, this last thing, I want you to know that I didn't steal this. But I did get a very good deal on it." Nino pulled a small jewelry box from his pocket and opened it revealing a three-carat diamond engagement ring. "And I really want you to marry me. Are you okay with that?"

Phyllis did not answer. She starred at the ring and then began to cry.

"Oh, no. Come on don't cry. What's the matter?"

"Nino, I'm sorry. I lied too. I'm not who you think I am."

"Don't tell me that."

"What? You think you're the only one who has to put a few extra decorations on the tree?"

"No, no. It's okay. What don't I know?"

Phyllis took a deep breath before saying, "I'm not Ricky's sister. I'm his mother."

A million questions popped into Nino's mind starting with Who, What, Where, and When. But instead of asking any of those he asked himself; did he really care? Would it really matter?

"Okay with that," Nino said. "Ricky and I like each other. He's a great kid. We make a great family. Marry me."

"I would love to marry you."

Nino took the ring from the box and slipped it on Phyllis' finger just as Joey Sclafani arrived at the booth.

"Joey, I'm getting married."

"Oh my god!" Joey signaled to a nearby captain. "Nunzio, champagne for the house." Then turning to the table, "Look at you two. What a beautiful couple. I'm going to have Pop make you something special for dessert."

As Joey walked away, Phyllis noticed that Nino was deep in thought. "What's up?"

"I'm just thinking about Ricky. He thinks your mother is his mother. You think this will screw him up?"

"When he's older and can understand he'll know the truth. And come on, he's going to live with two therapists. He'll get over it."

"You don't know, I was so afraid to tell you the truth. I thought for sure I was going to lose you."

"When I had to tell my father that I was pregnant I was so sure he was going to kick me out of the house. But he didn't. You know what he said? He said, 'Everybody has their line in the sand. If you cross that line, it's over, or it's war.' Then he said that I didn't cross that line in the sand and he loved me. Well, I love you, Nino Lombardo. And none of the things you told me cross my line in the sand."

"So what is that line?"

"You'll know when you cross it. But here's the other thing I've been thinking. So many people are getting divorced all of a sudden. I think we should have an office together and specialize in helping couples. Between my, 'what's your line in the sand,' and your, 'you just gotta do what you just gotta do,' I think we got something."

A waiter, followed by Joey Sclafani, arrived with flutes of champagne. The newly engaged couple raised their glasses as Joey addressed the room.

"Ladies and gentlemen, I propose a toast. To this beautiful couple, may they know a long life filled with health, happiness, and *familia*."

The entire restaurant erupted, "*Salude.*"

As Joey walked away Phyllis said, "You know Joey's not going to treat you like this anymore."

"Are you kidding me? You have no idea how screwed up Joey is. I'll have him in therapy for the rest of his life."

They touched glasses and drank.

TWENTY-FOUR

Henri Bouchet cut a small piece of his famous Brie, spread it on a slice of apple, and took a bite as he watched Armand struggle at his drafting table. Armand took yet another sketch, balled it up, and threw it at the wastebasket. A new day hadn't brought fresh ideas. Instead, Armand felt his unyielding mental block becoming more formidable. Frustration and fear prevented any creativity from coming to the forefront.

"You are wasting you time, Armand. You should be out looking for your new lover."

"*Fermez la bouche*. And eat your cheese."

"That is what's different in your life. That had to be your inspiration."

Armand tried to begin another sketch. He closed his eyes hoping for a vision; a neckline, a hemline, something, anything. There was nothing. He almost felt relief when his thoughts were interrupted by a soft knock on the door. It opened slightly and Tippy's head appeared.

"Excuse me, but there's no one out here. Have you seen Mickey?"

Armand sprung from his drafting table. "Tippy! *Bonjour*. Welcome. Come in." Armand went to Tippy as she entered his office. "How is the apartment? Are you getting settled?"

"The apartment is great. And settled? I think it's going to take a few days."

"You must tell me whatever you need. I want you to fall in love with Paris." Armand took Tippy's hand and kissed it. "And this is my brother, Henri."

Henri walked to Tippy, shook her hand and gave a slight bow. "*Bonjour, Madam*."

"*Bonjour*," Tippy said with a slightly confused look on her face.

"Is something wrong?" Henri asked.

"I'm sorry. But, that's very interesting cologne."

"It's brie. I smell like brie."

"Oh."

"Thank you."

"Tippy and Mickey are the people from America," Armand explained.

"Well, welcome to Paris. Brie?" Henri offered.

"No thank you." Tippy faced Armand and explained, "I was supposed to meet Mickey for lunch. I hope he didn't forget."

Once Tippy was facing Armand, Henri began to signal him that Tippy might be the perfect married woman to cast as his new muse.

"Actually he did tell me this morning that he was going out for lunch. Maybe there was some confusion," Armand suggested.

"You know, I have an idea," Henri said. "Perhaps you two should go to lunch. Armand could show you one of his favorite cafes."

"I don't know..."

"Henri is right. Let's do it. You are here to see Paris aren't you?"

"I thought I was."

"Then you should see it with a Frenchman. And I should be seen with a beautiful woman on my arm. Come. I will not take 'No' for an answer."

Armand wrapped Tippy's arm around his and led her out of his office. He quickly walked her across the factory floor and out the door just missing Mickey and Charlotte who had been working in the showroom area.

"I don't want to hear it, Mickey."

"I'm sorry, but I can't get out tonight. I haven't spent any time with Tippy since we got here."

"You're coming over. And I'm not talking about any quickies either. Last night was horrible. I want some time."

Before Mickey could reply, Henri approached.

"Are you Mickey?"

"Yeah."

"I am Henri. Armand's brother."

"Nice meeting you." Then it dawned on Mickey, "Hey you're the guy who stole…"

Henri interrupted, "Yes. And you're the guy who bought… So let's not get too righteous. Your wife called. She won't be able to make it for lunch. Nice meeting you."

Mickey watched Henri walk away. He was actually looking forward to lunch with Tippy. But perhaps he could make the disappointing circumstances work to his favor.

"Hey, instead of your place tonight, why don't we go there for lunch?"

"I don't think so," Charlotte said.

"Okay. How about as treat we go out for lunch? You're always complaining that we never go out in public." Charlotte hesitated before admitting, "Actually, I can't."

"Why not?"

"Well, I'm having lunch with someone."

"Who? Who do you know?"

"I'm having lunch with…with a neighbor…woman…old neighbor woman from…my neighbor."

Before Mickey could ask any more questions, Charlotte gave him a quick kiss on the cheek and ran out the door.

～

Having finished a light lunch at a nearby café, Tippy and Armand made their way across the Seine on the Pont Notre Dame.

"I can't believe how beautiful it all is. It's good to be awake for a change." Tippy wasn't sure if it was the sun on her face, or the beauty of Paris, or simply having a drug free mind, but she felt exhilarated.

"You don't seem like a woman who would sleep through life," Armand said.

"I'm not. But people back home…men mostly…and my mother, were worried that I was going crazy because I want to work. So they put me on these horrible pills to calm me down. I don't know what they're afraid of."

"Not all men think that's crazy."

Tippy looked to Armand to see if he was serious. He met her gaze and noticed something he first noticed over lunch; Tippy had fantastic hazel eyes.

"Are you familiar with the writing of Simone de Bouvoir?" he asked.

"Fraid not."

"A very strong French woman. In 1949 she wrote *The Second Sex*. It is about the American woman and her restlessness. It is very natural. Nothing that you should take a pill for."

"Wow, you get it."

"I hope so. In my work I must know what women feel, what they want, what they need, you know, emotionally." Armand was amazed he could deliver the line with a straight face. He had used it to seduce women of many nationalities. But American women, they were the ones who wanted the most from life.

Tippy stopped to take in the beauty of the fabulous Cathedral.

"I can't believe I'm seeing Notre Dame. It's amazing."

"I can't believe that Mickey hasn't taken you on a tour of the most romantic city in the world. You have not yet enjoyed the night life?"

"Nope. No, every night Mickey likes to go for a walk by himself."

"Every night?"

"Just about."

"Too bad. This is a very exciting city."

"I'm sure it is for you, being on top of the fashion world."

"I am nowhere near the top." As they continued their stroll Armand said, "The truth is; the fashion world is lonely. Yes I go to glamorous parties, to openings, to shows, to galas, but not with someone special. I should take you to one of the parties."

It had been so long since anyone had made a pass at Tippy she didn't even recognize it. "Mickey's not really a going to party kind of guy," she said. "He used to be, but not any more."

"Then I should take just you," Armand said.

"Right. Just what you want, a New York housewife."

Armand stopped walking. He turned to face Tippy. "What are you saying? Believe me, the women at these parties, they are no more beautiful than you."

The comment hit its mark. Tippy wasn't sure what to make of it. She blushed before saying, "Maybe we should be getting back."

"*Certainment.* But that's an open invitation."

They turned around and headed back across the bridge. As they passed a small park they didn't notice the couple enjoying a picnic on the grass.

Charlotte and Paul had their picnic lunch spread out on a blanket. Paul, in his mechanic's overalls, played his guitar and sang sweetly to Charlotte. He sang in French making it all the more enchanting.

"Paul, that was so beautiful."

"I felt inspired."

They sat quietly for a moment. Charlotte felt calm. She felt at ease.

"Perhaps you'd like to come to the coffee house where I sing sometimes." Paul said.

"Sure."

"Tonight?"

"I can't. I'm...I can't," Charlotte said as she played with a blade of grass.

"Tomorrow night?" Paul asked.

"I don't think so."

"Oh, I get it. You don't go out with an auto mechanic. I am a man with dirty hands."

"No. That's not it. You have...actually I was noticing that you have very nice hands. It's just that I shouldn't."

"You are seeing someone?"

"Sort of."

"Sort of? That means sort of yes and sort of no. No?"

"I guess."

"Then make tomorrow night a sort of no. Come on. I'm not going to bite you."

Charlotte thought about what she'd tell Mickey. She figured he'd probably be relieved that she wasn't demanding another night together. Her thoughts interrupted when Paul added, "Please."

"Okay."

"*Tres Bien*! I can't wait."

Paul leaned over and kissed Charlotte, first on one cheek and then the next. Then their eyes met. He quickly kissed her on the lips.

"I didn't know that came with a kiss on the lips," she said.

"It is an old trick. Every French boy uses it to get a kiss from his first love. It works, no?"

"It works, yes." She said with a smile.

TWENTY-FIVE

Mickey sat at Armand's drafting table doodling an imaginary model wearing his version of a sexy negligee. Unfortunately being exposed to Charlotte's never ending array of sex costumes was having its affect on his sense of style. As he drew, he felt compelled to add twin aircraft propellers to the drawing where nipples might be and added an old-fashioned leather flight helmet atop the drawing's featureless head. Lost in the creative process, Mickey didn't notice when Armand entered the office. It was only after signing "Michelle Daniel" to the sketch with a flourish that he saw Armand.

"Well, what have we here?" Armand asked as he walked over to the drafting table.

"I'm just messing around," Mickey said while covering the drawing as best he could. Armand still got a good peek.

"Michelle Daniel you have a very original fantasy life. This is your idea of a sexy woman? Perhaps you should leave the designing to me."

"I'd like to leave the designing to you," Mickey said. He tore the sketch off the large pad and balled it up. "But where the hell are the designs?"

"I'm working on them. Now, if you'll excuse me." Armand directed Mickey away from his work area.

As Mickey got up he asked, "And where's the money you said you were going to lend me? I've got to send some money back to the Mob."

"I was quite clear. As soon as you start production of the spring line, you will get the money."

"Yeah, well we need sketches for that."

"I said I'm working on them. In fact, I hope to have a breakthrough tonight, Michelle." Armand gave a sly laugh. As Mickey left

Armand's office, the laugh had Mickey wondering what the Frenchman was up to.

∼

Had Mickey stayed home that night he would have found out what Armand had planned. Instead, after an unsettling argument with Tippy who claimed to have come to the factory to meet Mickey for lunch, while he claimed that Armand's brother said that Tippy had called to cancel lunch, Mickey left his Paris townhouse and walked quickly down the street toward Charlotte's apartment. In his haste he failed to notice the man waiting in the darkened alley three doors down from Mickey and Tippy's pied-a-terre. As soon as Mickey walked past the alley, the man stepped out from the darkness and walked toward the Daniels' house.

Tippy sat at the kitchen table debating whether the move to Paris had been a huge mistake. She made a "Do It/Don't Do It" list. "Should she go back to New York" was the question at hand. Things in Paris weren't any different than how they were in New York. She was still sitting home, bored and without any prospects. Mickey wasn't making enough of an effort to re-connect. All reasons that suggested she should leave immediately. On the other hand, she didn't know when she might get back to Paris again. She could give things another few weeks and use the time to explore the city on her own. A good reason to be patient.

Her thoughts were interrupted by the doorbell.

"Armand!"

"*Bon soir*. I was just out walking and had a question for Mickey. Is he in?"

"No. You just missed him."

"What a shame. I was going to see if the two of you would like to join me for a glass of wine."

"Sorry. Sounds like fun."

"Would you like to join me?"

"No thanks."

"Please. It's not fun going alone."

"I'm not exactly dressed for a night on the town," she said. Although it wasn't as if she was lounging around in one of her many housecoats. Tippy was wearing a white cotton blouse with black Capri pants. Angelic white and devilish black, the contrast was exciting. The loose, flowing blouse gave only a hint of her beauty, the form fitting Capris accentuated her shapely legs.

"You look lovely. Really. Come on. It's a beautiful night. Why sit home alone?"

Armand had hit a chord. Why sit home alone, indeed? It was what Tippy had been doing all too often over the past months.

"What the hell?" she said. Tippy grabbed her purse and coat and headed into the Paris night with Armand.

TWENTY-SIX

Mickey and Charlotte sat cuddled on her sofa watching TV. He in his boxer shorts, she wearing a nightie that was once covered with a multitude of colored feathers but now, after a rather rough and tumble session together, looked more like a badly molting parrot.

"Can we go out, Mickey? This is so boring."

"What are you talking about? This is a terrific show."

"You don't understand a word their saying."

"What's to understand? The guy with the evil laugh is the bad guy and the guy with the happy laugh is the good guy."

Charlotte moved away from Mickey and watched quietly for a minute.

"I have a date tomorrow night," she said.

"I'm not sure I can get out tomorrow."

"No, Mickey. I have a date tomorrow."

"With a guy?"

She hated his tone which implied that was an impossibility.

"Yes, with a guy."

"A French guy?"

"Yeah."

"Just like that?"

"It's not just like that. I'm going to hear a neighbor sing."

"The old woman?"

"Look, if you don't want me to go, I won't."

Mickey didn't answer right away. He wondered if he cared if she went. Charlotte didn't wait for his answer.

"I'm just confused. I want more, Mickey."

"Look, Charlotte..."

Mickey hesitated, not sure of what to say. He had never really examined his true feelings for Charlotte. Did he have any? If he thought about how he felt about Charlotte, what would that mean for his marriage to Tippy? It was all too confusing. He found himself speechless.

"I know this isn't easy for you. But there's something I want you to read." Charlotte got up from the couch and walked to the small dresser that sat next to her bed. As she walked she left a trail of the few remaining feathers. She opened the top drawer and took out a folded note. Returning to the couch she explained, "I wrote this to you because writing it down helps me figure things out. I'm trying to figure out why I'm confused. I'm trying to figure out how I really feel."

"I know how you feel."

"No you don't. Not really. Just read it."

"I don't need to."

"Mickey, please."

"I don't need to."

There was nothing more to say. Mickey went back to watching French TV. Charlotte took the note and walked toward the dresser stopping only to slip the note into the pocket of Mickey's sport coat.

TWENTY-SEVEN

~~~~~

Le Cul de Chat bistro was packed with young hip Parisians standing three deep at the bar. A jukebox blasting Johnny Hallyday singing French rock and roll added to the din.

Tippy and Armand were squeezed together at a tiny table for two. They watched their waiter make yet another attempt at opening a bottle of wine. Each time he'd try to insert the corkscrew, he was jostled by the crowd.

"Is it always this crowded here?" Tippy asked, raising her voice to a low holler.

"I usually go to a quiet little café, but I thought you'd like to see some of the Paris excitement," Armand said. "We won't stay too long. Let's have a glass of wine and then I want to take you to a party."

"A party? No. You can just drop me off."

"Why?"

"I'm not dressed for a party."

"It's just a few friends. Very casual. You'll have fun. I promise.

The waiter, having successfully opened the bottle, stood his ground while Armand sampled the wine. He nodded his approval and the waiter poured a glass for Tippy and for Armand.

Armand raised his glass. "To you. May you discover all the excitement and romance that Paris has to offer."

"That would be nice."

They touched glasses and took a sip of wine. Before Tippy could get her glass back on the table, a woman trying to squeeze through the crowd bumped into her spilling red wine all over Tippy's white blouse. The woman ignored Tippy's scream and continued on her way without even a perfunctory "*Pardon.*"

"Look at this. It'll never come out. Look, you go to your party. I'll get home."

"Tippy, take off your blouse."

"I beg your pardon."

"You are wearing a brassiere, no?"

"Yes."

"Then take off your blouse."

"I don't think so."

"I will fix your blouse. Tippy, I would never do anything to embarrass you. Believe me. This is Paris. No one will notice."

Tippy froze, not sure what to do. Removing her blouse in a crowded bar was not something she'd normally consider. But Armand seemed so sincere in his promise not to embarrass her. And this was Paris after all. She slowly unbuttoned her blouse. She took it off. Immediately the entire bistro fell silent. Even the jukebox, no longer full of francs fell silent.

"No one will notice?"

"I didn't think you would do it," Armand admitted with a smile. He spread her blouse on the table, dipped his napkin in to his glass of red wine, and began to dab the soaked napkin onto the blouse. Each time he dabbed the blouse a red flower appeared. The entire room was no longer staring at Tippy. They were mesmerized by the artist at work. Once he was satisfied with the blouse, Armand made larger wine colored flowers on the tablecloth. When he finished with that he held out Tippy's blouse for her to put on. She slipped her arms in. Armand began to button it for her. He was standing close. Very close. He only buttoned a few of the middle buttons. He tied her shirttails calypso style leaving her with a bare midriff.

"You have a very lovely navel," he whispered.

"You said you weren't going to embarrass me."

Armand stepped back and admired his work for a moment. Then he moved the wine bottle, the glasses, and a small vase to an adjacent table. He removed the tablecloth and tied it around Tippy's waist forming it into a Tahitian style pareo. Again he stepped back.

"Do you know how you can tell a real designer?" he asked.

"How?"

"His greatest joy is taking a beautiful woman and making her more beautiful." To finish his creation, Armand plucked a fresh rose from the bud vase and placed it in Tippy's hair. She was stunning.

"Voila!" he said triumphantly.

The bistro exploded with applause, the patrons having been witness to a master at work.

Armand threw a few francs on the table then offered his arm to Tippy. She took it and they walked triumphantly, arm-in-arm out, into the Paris night.

It was late into the night when Tippy and Armand approached her building. They were both still a little drunk. She still looked like she had stepped out of the pages of Paris Vogue in her wine stained ensemble. They stopped once they arrived at the steps leading up to her door.

"I had a great time, Armand. Thank you."

"No, thank you. I had a great time as well."

They stood silently for a moment. In some ways Tippy did not want the night to end. It had been so long since she'd had this much fun.

"Well, good night," she said.

"Good night, Tippy." Armand leaned in and kissed her on one cheek and then the other. Then, after holding her at arms length for a moment, he kissed her lips. She didn't resist at first but then broke away.

"Don't do that," she said softly.

"Forgive me. *Bon soir*, Tippy. *Bon soir*." Armand walked off into the night.

Tippy made it to her bedroom where she stood admiring her wine-stained outfit in the mirror. She had to admit, she did look beautiful in it. She modeled it for herself but stopped abruptly when she heard the front door close.

"Mickey?"

"Yeah. I'm back."

Tippy quickly unwrapped the skirt and pulled the blouse over her head t-shirt style and threw them in the hamper before Mickey got to the bedroom.

"Sorry I'm so late. I lost track of the time."

Instead of questioning him, she said, "That's okay. I'm going to take a shower."

Once in the bathroom, she turned on the water. As the shower warmed up, Tippy stared at herself in the mirror and ran her fingers over her lips.

The next morning, while cleaning the bedroom, Tippy picked up the jacket Mickey had worn the night before and was about to go through the pockets when the phone rang.

"Hello."

"*Bonjour*, Tippy, it's Armand."

"Hi, Armand. Mickey isn't here."

"I'm not calling Mickey. I'm calling you. I just wanted to thank you for the lovely time last night."

"It was a very nice evening," she said matter-of-factly. She was determined to sound as business like as possible in spite of the huge smile on her face.

"Yes, but I feel guilty. I promised you a cup of coffee and we never had it. So I was wondering if you'd like to meet me for coffee tonight."

"No. I don't think so," she said.

"Why not?"

"Why not? I'm a married woman. I don't think I should be dating."

"It's not a date. It's coffee with a friend. What could be more innocent?"

"No. I'm afraid not."

"Well, if you change your mind, I'll be at Café Jacqueline on Rue Lois Blanc. I would love to see you."

"It's not going to happen, Armand. But thank you. Bye bye."

Tippy hung up the phone and got back to work. She took a hanger from the closet and was about to hang up Mickey's jacket when she remembered to check the pockets since Mickey was always losing important papers, and they most often were in his pockets. Sure enough, there was a folded paper. Tippy took it out and unfolded it. She began to read the letter from Charlotte. She sat on her bed and began to cry as she continued to read.

TWENTY-EIGHT

After a long day with no designs coming from Armand, Mickey walked toward the apartment, a bouquet of flowers in hand. He had decided earlier in the afternoon that once and for all he would end his affair. He had never had a problem wheeling and dealing. Telling the occasional lie to a customer about the country of origin of a housecoat, or how a shipment of goods was late because the government had commandeered it in order to send housecoats to the wives of Eastern European communists in some sort of cockamamie radio-free-housecoats-from-America program in an effort to win the cold war was never a problem for Mickey. He was always able to add a very sincere, "I swear to God," to the most outrageous of lies. But the lying to Tippy was different. It ate at him in a way he could no longer stand. The two dozen roses he carried would be the peace offering that would be followed by a romantic night on the town in Paris. All Mickey could think about as he entered their apartment was starting a new chapter with Tippy.

"Tippy? Look what I got for you," he called out. "Do we have a vase?"

His question was answered as it was indeed a vase that went whizzing by his head before it crashed against the door. Tippy looked around for something else to throw.

"What are you doing?" Mickey asked.

Tippy stopped her search. She stood, hands on hips as she began her tirade. "You son-of-a-bitch. Night after night I sat wondering what was wrong with me. What did I need to do to fix things? What could I do to make things better? And what were you doing? You were busy screwing your secretary."

"What are you talking about?" Mickey asked, denial being his first instinct.

"Don't play dumb." Tippy held out the note from Charlotte. "This is what I'm talking about. Why'd you have to drag me to Paris? I could have been happy selling hot dogs in New York."

"Tip, it just happened. I wanted to stop but..."

"But what? You didn't have the courage? Well you don't have to. We're through."

"Tippy, I love you. I swear to God."

"Yeah, well, I only wish I didn't love you."

Tippy grabbed the flowers from Mickey's hands, threw them to the floor, then rushed out of the apartment. For the next few hours she roamed the streets of Paris unaware of the time. She would cry until there were no more tears. The tears would be replaced by rage until more tears returned. The tears were prompted by the sight of couples in love, a seemingly unavoidable sight in the City of Love. Every street seemed to have a couple kissing in the shadows. Every sidewalk café infested with couples whispering sweet nothings in each others' ears. An elderly couple in a park walked hand in hand until they reached an unoccupied bench. The old man took a handkerchief from his pocket and lovingly wiped the bench clean before allowing his love to sit down. He put his arm around the old woman and they snuggled close. Tippy could not escape. She soon found a bench of her own and spent another hour simply watching happy couples go by.

∽

Charlotte and Paul were singing "Alouette," as they walked arm-in-arm down the street toward her apartment.

He sang, *"Je te plumerai la tete,"* while pointing to Charlotte's head.

She responded with, "Gentle plumber's A la tet," in perhaps the worst attempt at French ever.

It made Paul laugh as he sang, *"Et la tete."*

"Hey la tet."

"Aluette."

"Al's all wet."

Then in unison they sang the only part she got right. "Ooohhhh-hh..."

They were both laughing when they arrived at Charlotte's door. Having finished their song Charlotte searched for her key.

"I had a great time tonight."

"Our evening is over?" he asked. "It is so early. Would you like to come to my place for coffee?"

"I better not," she said unlocking her door.

"Okay. But I had a great time too. I want to see you again. Maybe dinner tomorrow?"

Charlotte hesitated before whispering almost to herself, "I'm not sure."

"Not sure? *Pourquoi?* Why? Is this Mr. Sort Of again?"

Charlotte stood silently, not wanting to answer. Paul took her hand.

"Charlotte, you are having an affair with a married man, no?"

"No."

"Please. The French know these things."

"Well, okay, I am. But I'm confused about it. And...I don't know... maybe we should wait until I figure it out."

"If that's what you want, fine. But I cannot wait. And neither can true love. You see, you might decide to stay in this hell for a long, long time."

"It's not exactly hell," she said, taking her hand from his. She wasn't sure she wanted this uninvited appraisal of her relationship with Mickey.

As she opened her door, Paul challenged her. "Not hell? Really? Let me tell you about being the other woman. I know this because..."

"The French just know these things," she blurted out with a bit more attitude than she planned.

"No. I have other friends who are kept women and I see their pain. And worse, I see their lack of joy. It makes me mad. Wonderful beautiful women, like you, who are willing to wait for these men. Hoping he will call. Accepting the scraps of emotional moments that are thrown to them. They tell me, 'You don't understand, Paul. The sex, it is wild.

Like nothing I can have anywhere else.' That is because it is the sex of desperation. It is a performance of This Is What You Would Get If We Were Together All The Time. But it is without true love. And so it is empty. And true love is what you deserve, Charlotte. That is what I want for you."

Charlotte looked into his eyes for a moment to make sure she had not just heard a line. A man had never looked at her before with so much love. She kissed him passionately. He took her in his arms. While holding the embrace she kicked the door open. She grabbed his ass. He grabbed her ass and they stumbled into her apartment.

TWENTY-NINE

An uncomfortable silence hung between Armand and Claude LeMonde as they watched their waiter open a bottle of wine. After a taste and a nod from LeMonde the waiter poured a glass of wine for each of them before disappearing into the smoke filled café. Armand lifted his glass to LeMonde who, instead of returning the gesture, simply took a drink. The wine was barely satisfactory but LeMonde was not about to spend a fortune on good wine considering the news he was about to deliver. Even though he enjoyed being part of the glamorous world of fashion, like most investors, a healthy bottom line was his real motivation. With disappointing sales from Armand's Winter line and still no sketches for the upcoming Spring show LeMonde was not prepared to throw good money after bad.

"So, Armand, I'm sorry but your time is up. If I do not see sketches by nine o'clock tomorrow morning I'm afraid the House of Armand will exist no more."

The world of fashion is built on fantasy and illusion. Armand had no intention of joining LeMonde in this particular reality. "The house of Armand will always exist," Armand said defiantly.

"Perhaps. But not with my money behind it."

Armand did his best to remain calm. "Claude, believe me. I have a new inspiration driving my work. A new muse. This new woman is fantastic. She will inspire me to new heights."

"C'est bon. She has until nine o'clock tomorrow."

Calm had not worked. Armand was about to switch to outright begging when he spotted Tippy at the front of the café speaking with the Maitre D. "In that case, Claude, you must leave."

"*Pourquoi?*"

"Because I must go to work," Armand explained just as the Maitre D lead Tippy to the table.

As soon as she saw that Armand was not alone Tippy felt her face redden. What was she doing here? She really wasn't sure. She wanted to run, to be alone with her anger and confusion. But it was too late. Armand was standing now, welcoming her.

"Tippy, I'm so glad you decided to come."

"I'm sorry, Armand. I didn't know you'd be with someone."

"No, no, no. Claude was just having a drink and then leaving,"

"Yes, I must be on my way," LeMonde said as he stood, then offered Tippy his seat. She felt she had no choice but to sit. Before heading off into the night LeMonde added, "Good luck, Armand. I can see why you expect great things. *Au revoir."*

Armand signaled for the waiter to bring a clean glass then looked directly into Tippy's eyes. "I'm thrilled to see you. This is a very pleasant surprise."

"I had to get out of the house."

Armand took Tippy's hand before asking, "Is something wrong?"

Tippy's anger had quashed her self-control. She was prepared to tell the world of Mickey's betrayal. "I just found out that Mickey's been having an affair. I don't know what to do."

"Maybe you should have an affair," he suggested as he put his free hand on top of hers.

She immediately pulled her hand back. "Maybe I should what?"

Armand took a sip of wine to slow things down. He didn't want to seem panicked. "Maybe you should have an affair too. Add some romance to your life."

Tippy shook her head in disbelief. "Boy, and I thought you got it. An affair? That's what I need? Another man is your idea of what will give me more out of life? Another man will make me forget that my marriage is falling apart? Have an affair? You're all the same, aren't you?"

Armand remained calm. He knew how to handle the situation. He leaned in toward her. "Excuse me. I believe you want more control of your life, don't you? Well I am not talking about an affair where you wait submissively for a man at his beck and call. Wondering if today is the day he can sneak away and take you to new heights of ecstasy, no matter how exciting that might be. I'm talking about an affair where you are in control. This would be you, a modern woman, making decisions for herself about her life. About her body. This would be you being the predator, not some taken-for-granted housewife. I am talking about you having sex for sex's sake. Just like a man. I'm talking about an excitement like you have never known. You and your lover thrilling each other with every touch. Rediscovering a passion you thought was gone forever but still burns brightly deep within. That's what I thought you wanted. But I guess you do not find the prospect of being a strong, truly independent woman so appealing. Forgive me for misreading you so badly." Armand stood and walked away from the table. After a few steps he stopped, returned to Tippy, and added, "If, however, you change your mind, I find you fascinating." Then he turned and walked away.

She called to him while he was still in earshot. He stopped and waited. Tippy got up from the table, took Armand's hand and they headed off into the Paris night together.

THIRTY

Charlotte and Paul lay next to each other, both still panting. They each wore a red plastic fireman's hat. Paul held a stuffed Dalmatian under one arm and kept Charlotte close with the other. Finally catching his breath, Paul asked, "That was incredible. What did you call that again?"

"That's a hook and ladder," she whispered.

"And I thought the French knew about these things."

They both laughed then Paul leaned in and kissed her. They held the kiss even though the phone began to ring. After a few rings though, when it became obvious that the ringing wasn't going to stop, Paul asked, "Aren't you going to answer that?"

"No," Charlotte said before resuming the kiss. Still, the ringing would not stop.

Paul broke away again and asked, "Why?"

"There are only two people who call me in Paris, and one of them is in bed with me. And one...I don't want to talk to right now." Charlotte pulled Paul back to her and kissed him again. The phone, however, kept up its incessant ringing. Finally she could take no more. She grabbed the bedside receiver. "What?"

Mickey didn't ask why she took so long to answer or why her greeting was so curt. He got right down to business. "I need to see you." There was no response from Charlotte. "Tippy found your note." There was still nothing from Charlotte. Mickey's frustration grew. "Look, Charlotte, I need to talk to someone. I need to talk to you."

Mickey sounded desperate, like he really did need to talk with her. Charlotte took a deep breath before telling Mickey, "I can't. Look, Mickey, you've wanted to end this for a long time. You didn't really want to bring me to Paris in the first place. I explained all this. Did you read the note?"

"No, but my wife sure has."

"It said that I never wanted to make you miserable. I understand how you feel. But I insisted in coming here because I wanted to find my true love. Well...I think I have."

Charlotte looked at Paul. She let the phone drop to the bed before falling into his arms. They paid no attention to Mickey's muffled yelling about why he needed to talk or that he was coming right over.

Mickey was not about to be ignored. He slammed the phone down, grabbed his jacket and stormed out of the apartment without bothering to lock it.

He got one arm through a jacket sleeve as he took the front steps two by two. He was just getting the second arm into a sleeve as he passed the adjacent alley. In his haste, he never saw the huge arm that reached out and pulled him off the street. It all happened so quickly he had no idea who or what slammed into his stomach so hard that it doubled him over. And in that position he certainly didn't see the powerful punch to the jaw that knocked him out.

"Mickey, are you okay? Mick? Shit." Nino stood over Mickey's lifeless body. He hadn't really meant to knock him unconscious but his frustration got the best of him. He tried lightly slapping Mickey's face a few times in an attempt to bring him to. It was no luck. He was out cold.

Nino picked Mickey up into his arms and carried him back to the apartment. He laid Mickey on the couch then found his way to the kitchen. He took a dishtowel, wet it, got a handful of ice from the refrigerator, and made a cold compress. Nino carefully put it on Mickey's forehead just as he began to stir.

"Jesus, Mickey, are you okay?"

Mickey strained to bring the world back into focus. He wasn't sure if he was seeing straight through the mental cobwebs. "Nino?"

"Hey, Mick."

"Are you going to kill me?"

"Yeah. Are you okay?"

"I guess." Mickey sat up slowly. He removed the impromptu ice bag from his head and moved it to his jaw which was now beginning to throb. "Listen, you don't have to kill me. I'm going to get you your money."

"You think I give a shit about the money? I can't believe you just left me to hang out to dry with my old man. What kind of friend does that?"

"I had to. It was the only way to pay you back."

"Yeah, right."

"Sit down, would you?"

Nino hesitated, trying to decide if he wanted to hear this or not. If there was no good explanation for Mickey's behavior he really would have to kill him or at least permanently maim him to satisfy his father. He sat down on the couch. "This better be good."

"Look, Armand said he'd give me the money to pay you back if I came to Paris to get his line out. He was going to help me get everything straightened out. You, Tippy, Charlotte, me in the fashion business, everything. Now you hate me, Charlotte's with someone else, and worst of all, Tippy's leaving me." Suddenly Mickey felt a pain that was much worse than his throbbing jaw. Tears began to run down his face. "She's leaving me, Nino. I thought it was all going to work out. It was perfect. There was no risk."

"Would you shut the fuck up with this no risk bullshit? You want to be in the fashion business? Stop cutting corners. Come up with an idea. Take a risk. You want to save your marriage? Go beg Tippy to come back. Show her what she fell in love with in the first place. Take a risk. How can you be so stupid? No risk. What a crock of shit."

"I thought it would work. You don't know what I'm going through."

"I know plenty, Mickey. I see people at their worst and their weakest. I see them when they're about to get beat up or have a leg broken. I see them when they're begging for mercy. Not all of them. Some try to be tough. But eventually that smart ones figure out that you have to face the music. That's what you're up to, Buddy Boy."

They sat quietly for a moment. Mickey tried to picture a future where everything worked out. It wouldn't come into focus. "You're not really going to kill me, are you?"

"Yes. Yes. Yes. And it's your fucking fault. God, I hate doing this." Nino made a fist. He wanted to punch someone, something, anything to drain his rage. "I'm going to kill you all right. We just have to figure out how."

"We? I have to help?"

"What is with you? You always think you're the only one who needs help."

"I'm sorry," Mickey said. "I really am. Don't worry. We'll come up with something."

THIRTY-ONE

With the covers pulled up to her chin, Tippy watched Armand, now dressed in a bathrobe, sitting at his drafting table, drawing like a madman. For the past fifteen minutes, ever since they finished having the most mechanical sex Tippy had ever experienced, Armand would quickly do a sketch and then tear it up and begin swearing in French.

"Merd! Merd! Merd! Merd! Merd!"

"What's wrong now?" she asked with a soupcon of irritation in her voice. The Frenchman was beginning to sound a bit whiney and emotionally she felt numb.

"There's still nothing happening. Perhaps we should make love again."

"No." Tippy was sure that was not what she needed.

"But it was wonderful. No?"

"I don't know. No. I was just getting back at Mickey. I need to get back to New York." Although now slightly embarrassed, Tippy got out of bed and began gathering her clothes from the floor.

"Please, Tippy, you are my inspiration. I need you to inspire my new line."

"What are you talking about?" Tippy asked as she covered her nakedness as best she could by hugging her wrinkled dress.

"Please stay the night. You can sleep. Alone. Let me draw you. You can't fly back to New York until morning. Please."

Tippy thought for a moment. She didn't want to stay but she really didn't want to go back to the apartment and deal with Mickey. She would go back there in the morning, pack her things, and leave. "Okay," she said.

"Bless you." Armand began another sketch as Tippy got back into the bed.

∼

Armand wasn't the only one sketching to save his life. Having grown tired of sitting with Nino supposedly helping him think of ways for Nino to kill him, Mickey went to the kitchen table and began to draw. Nino's earlier advice to take a risk and design something made much more sense to Mickey than waiting for his friend to kill him. Unfortunately, Charlotte's influence was still all too evident in Mickey's work. He only felt inspired to create negligee and the one he was working on was being modeled by a Swiss milkmaid. He knew her metal pail wasn't the provocative touch he was looking for but he couldn't help himself. Just as he was putting the finishing touches on the sketch Nino entered the kitchen.

"I'm bushed. I gotta get some sleep." Then, noticing Mickey's work, he asked, "What's all this?"

"Crap. I guess that's all I know how to make," Mickey said as he tore up the drawing.

"Boo hoo. Stop your bellyaching. This isn't taking a risk. Take a risk, damn it. At least once before I kill you. Good night."

Nino left the kitchen to sleep on the couch. Mickey got back to work, determined to eliminate the cartoon characteristics of his previous attempts. As the night wore on he continued to hang his efforts around the kitchen. They continued to get better but not great. He tore them down and started drawing again. Within a few hours the kitchen walls were again strewn with drawings. Although unplanned, in each ensuing sketch, the face of the model had more and more detail. And in each drawing the face looked more and more like Tippy's. Still unhappy with the designs Mickey again tore down the sketches. It was three o'clock in the morning. He was exhausted. But he pressed on.

He wasn't sure when it was but suddenly there was an image in his mind. A vision of a flowing nightgown with a lace bodice that evoked sparklers on the Fourth of July came into focus. The sparkler-like lace was not cartoonish like his earlier efforts. It was alive with a sense of joy. It seemed to take only moments to get the vision onto paper. As soon as he finished it, a shorter, baby doll nightie came to mind. He began to draw as fast as he could. It was as if his hand could not keep up with his mind. He didn't know where the ideas were coming from, but it was like an avalanche. Silk pajamas with a cutaway top that revealed hip-hugging bottoms held up by the tiniest drawstring. Each drawing had a sense of elegance yet oozed seduction. Within fifteen minutes he had drawn an entire line of sleepwear.

Then came the slips and the camisoles. Each time a vision would come to mind he wished he could see it on Tippy. He wished he could hold her while caressing the fabric. What fabric? How would he make these fantasies come to life if he had the chance? He jotted notes in the margin of each sketch laying out fabric choices and color schemes.

On some level he knew how each garment should feel when worn. The feel: that was the most important thing. Women should feel beautiful. Women should feel desirable. No matter what they were wearing on top of one of his slips, inside, at their core, he wanted women to feel the power of their femininity.

Suddenly there were flashes of undies. Very, very, sexy undies. For a split second he worried that he was becoming some kind of obsessed pervert. What kind of man draws women's undies in the middle of the night? Mickey Daniels, that kind of guy. If he was a pervert so what? He couldn't wait to see them. So he drew and he drew. And even when he came up with a pair that looked like old-fashioned bloomers, there was something about them that was incredibly enticing.

And then it was robes, the rich, uptown cousin of the housecoat. When the first one came to mind he laughed out loud. Whomever or whatever was sending these ideas had a sense of humor. The joke didn't stop him. He kept sketching. These robes were nothing like the shmatas he schlepped from one lousy account to the next. They were works of art with detail work that said they were made by craftsmen. But no matter how elegant and tasteful, there was still something about each creation that would make a man want to tear them off and make love to the lucky woman who wore them.

Mickey didn't bother looking at his watch. Time meant nothing. He drew until there was no more wall space, no room on the refrigerator door, no cabinet door that didn't hold a fabulous sketch. Exhausted, he laid his head on the kitchen table and fell into a deep sleep.

It was only seven A.M. and Nino was still asleep on the couch when Tippy came home to gather her things. When she closed the door it woke him up.

"Hey, Tip."

"What are you doing here?"

"I came to kill Mickey."

"Good."

"How you doin'?"

"I've been better."

As Tippy started for the bedroom, Mickey came out from the kitchen. She stopped to explain, "I'm just here to get my things. I'm going back to New York."

"Tip, I'm sorry," Mickey said.

"Yeah, well so am I. Sorry I let you drag me here."

Nino wished that Phyllis was with him. Here was a couple in trouble. Together, he knew that they could help. Without her he'd have to go it solo. He decided to start with common sense. He got up from the couch and walked over to Tippy. "Can I ask you something, Tip? When you got married, how long did you think it was going to last?"

"Forever." Then turning to Mickey she added, "I guess I am stupid."

"If anyone's stupid it's me."

"Okay, I think we can all agree on that," Nino said. "You know, Tip, I remember at your wedding, you took each other for better or worse. What did you think 'worse' was?"

"I don't know," Tippy answered, the question had caught her off guard. "Maybe that he would walk around farting as much as my father does."

"That's not 'worse'. That's normal," Nino explained. "You know what I think? I think that this is the 'worse' they're talking about. This is it. They call it 'worse' because if they actually said that there's a chance that one of you may cheat on the other, then nobody would ever get married. So they call it 'worse'. But this is it."

"Look, you don't understand. You're not even married."

"No. But I'm getting married."

"Really?" Mickey asked.

"Yeah, really. You'd have known if you hadn't taken off behind my back," Then turning back to Tippy, Nino said, "I'm not married yet. But my parents have been married a long, long time. And I remember when I was kid they used to fight all the time. And even then, I knew what they were fighting about. They were going through what you are now. Well, all I know is somehow they got through it. And now...well now I'm afraid to go over there during the day. They can't keep their hands off each other. It's disgusting. But, you know what? I think they're going to be married forever."

"Good for them, Nino. But I'm never going to trust Mickey again."

"Hey, life is a test. Nobody gets a perfect paper. Not Mickey. Not you. Nobody. He fucked up. Can you trust him today? No. Tomorrow? Maybe. It depends if he keeps fucking up."

"I won't." Mickey chimed in.

Nino turned to him. "Shut up. You don't know that. I don't know that." Then turning back to face Tippy, Nino said, "But here's what I do know. He's my best friend. There are certain things he can't bullshit about. I know he loves you."

"It's true, Tip. And Nino knows people because of when he beats them up and all."

Nino felt he was getting close. It was time to go for the heavy hitters. He took Tippy's hands in his. "Everybody's got their line in the sand that they're not willing to cross. Maybe this is yours. If it is then you just gotta do what you just gotta do. But if it isn't your line in the sand...if there's something here worth saving..."

As Tippy considered what Nino had said he turned to Mickey. "You got any coffee?"

"Yeah."

Nino quickly turned his attention back to Tippy. "You want a cup?"

Tippy hesitated for a moment then, still holding one of Nino's hands, walked to the kitchen.

Tippy and Nino couldn't help but be impressed by the amount of work that hung in the kitchen. Every inch was covered with Mickey's sketches.

"You've been a busy boy," Nino said.

Mickey felt naked having them see his work. His real work. "Yeah, well you can tell I'm not a real designer. They're not very good."

Tippy kept looking, going from one drawing to the next. "Yes they are. They're sexy."

"That's what I was going for." Encouraged by her reaction he added, "They got better once I figured out the secret."

"You must have figured out something. These are so much better than that bullshit you were drawing last night," Nino said as he admired the sketch of a little, white, spaghetti strap nightie peeking out from an elegant peignoir.

"I just took the most beautiful woman I know and tried my hardest to make her more beautiful."

Tippy said nothing as she closely examined the sketch of what seemed to be sort of, but not quite a Teddy. It was the most discreetly naughty undergarment she had ever seen. "What's this thing for?"

"I'm not sure. It's for whatever."

Tippy closed her eyes, took a deep breath, and let out a sigh. With eyes still closed she said, "If we did try to make things work, there's a lot that has to change."

"Anything, Tip. Name it. You want a hot dog stand? You can have a hot dog stand. You want me to never go on walk by myself for as long as I live? I won't. Whatever. I don't want to lose you."

Tippy finally looked at Mickey. I don't want a hot dog stand.

"Okay." Mickey suspected there was more coming.

"I want to run the business."

"What business?" he asked.

"Your business. These drawings, they're great. We can sell these. But you stink at the business."

"I do not."

"You spend your time getting nickeled and dimed to death on the Lower East Side. You stink at it. I'm taking over the business."

"Jesus, she should be working for my old man," Nino said, trying to lighten things up. Tippy turned to him.

"And you tell your old man that we'll pay back what we owe, but not with twenty percent interest."

"How do you know about the money?" Mickey asked.

"Armand told me."

There was an uncomfortable silence as Mickey put together the possibilities of how and when Tippy might have been with Armand. Tippy took control of the situation.

"And Nino, you can't kill him unless I give you permission."

"I think I can go along with that."

Tippy took down a sketch from the refrigerator and began to roll it up. "Come on, get the rest of them," she ordered. "We've got to get going."

"Where?" Mickey asked as he carefully removed a sketch from a cabinet door.

Tippy walked over to Mickey. "We are going to do some business," she said. They stood there for a moment, Tippy looking into Mickey's eyes. Then she slapped him across the face. "Now let's go."

Tippy headed out of the kitchen followed by Nino. Mickey took one moment to absorb the sting, then gathered up the rest of the sketches.

THIRTY-TWO

Inside Armand's office, Henri Bouchet unwrapped a tray of artisan cheeses while Claude LeMonde toyed with his pocket watch. The antique timepiece yet another affectation intended to make him seem interesting rather than simply the heir to a small fortune.

"*C'est temp.* I cannot wait any longer. I told him he had until nine," LeMonde said as he stood and prepared to leave.

"He'll be here. Please sit. Have some cheese." Henri held out the tray in an attempt to block LeMonde's exit.

"The smell of that brie is making me nauseous," LeMonde said.

"I brought camembert. The brie is me."

"Actually it smells like very nice, ripe brie," LeMonde said to cover the insult.

"*Merci.*"

LeMonde checked his watch again. "But still, I have waited long enough. I don't think Armand is going to have the sketches."

LeMonde stood and headed for the door. Before he got there, though, it swung open. Armand, still in his bathrobe and in need of a morning shave, strode in, a roll of sketches under his arm.

"Voila! I have it," Armand announced triumphantly.

"Thank God," Henri said, popping a piece of cheese in his mouth to calm himself.

"I suppose two minutes late isn't too late," LeMonde said with a smile. "Let's see them."

As Armand hung a sketch on the large bulletin board behind his drafting table he explained, "I decided to go back to basics. That's what always works." Then with a flourish he announced, "I give you the simple black dress."

Claude LeMonde studied the sketch. It was indeed a simple black dress. Too simple. So simple that it wasn't the least bit interesting.

"That's it?" LeMonde asked.

Armand immediately felt a cool bead of sweat run from his armpit down his side. "Well it can come in different colors. You know a simple blue dress, a simple red dress."

LeMonde moved closer to the inept drawing just in case he was missing something. "Do you honestly think this is good? It's terrible."

Armand slumped into his chair and laid his head on his drafting table. "It is terrible, isn't it? I don't know what happened,"

Henri walked to the drafting table and laid a brotherly hand on Armand's shoulder. "It may be too soon, but just know that you can always make cheese with me. It may not be as glamorous as the fashion business but people are always complementing me on how I smell like very good brie."

Armand lifted his head and pleaded with LeMonde, "Please, Claude. Don't close me down."

Before LeMonde could answer there was a knock on the door and Tippy stuck her head in.

"Hi. Can I come in?"

"This isn't a good time, I'm afraid," Armand replied.

"Maybe it is. I think I have a solution to your problem. I'm guessing you didn't have a breakthrough."

"He did not," LeMonde answered.

Tippy took over the center of the room. She was in charge, feeling her full power. "Nino, would you please pin up the sketches."

As Nino walked to the bulletin board Armand asked, "Who's he?"

"One of the reasons I came over here was so that I could pay back the Mob." Mickey explained.

"So?"

"So I'm the Mob," Nino said.

"Welcome."

Tippy directed her attention to Claude LeMonde. "I know from my discussions with Armand that he's having trouble coming up with designs. So just for this show, why not have Armand present the work of an exciting new designer, Michelle Daniel?" Tippy said. "No one does lingerie like this. It's sexy, but classy. It screams, Take me. Take me now". Tippy's voice was at a low growl.

Mickey, besides being incredibly turned on by her performance, was also awed by a level of salesmanship that he could only dream of.

"I'm telling you," she continued, "both women and men will love it."

LeMonde walked to the sketches Nino had hung. He examined them closely. "This is very sexy."

"So sexy! I would love to have some of these drawings," Henri added.

"I don't think that's going to happen this time, Buddy Boy," Nino explained.

"These are very nice. But what about the next show? And the next?" LeMonde asked.

"He's right," moaned Armand. "This solves nothing. I can no longer design. I'm ruined."

"Hold it, Pal," Nino said. He walked over to Armand's drafting table. "You're still a great designer. But even the greatest artists get blocked sometimes. You'll be back."

"Do you really believe that?" Armand asked.

"Yeah. I do. And you know what? I think you believe it too," Nino said while giving Armand a gentle pat on the back.

"Yes, you should not give up," Henri added. "Forget the cheese business. You need to keep drawing."

Nino then turned to Henri. "And you should forget the cheese business too. We both know you've been doing some pretty crazy stuff. It's because you hate what you do. No one should do something they hate doing. Not you. Not Mickey. Not me. Nobody."

"Okay, that's it, Nino," Mickey said. "I mean I hate to break up this beautiful moment, but when did you become the big people expert? I mean you're giving advice to Tippy and me. You're giving advice to this guy and that guy. This isn't just 'I know people because I beat them up stuff.' And I'm not saying the advice is bad. It's good. But what gives?"

"You really want to know? Okay. One day I'm making my usual rounds and I go to collect from this psychology professor, Peter Ivanofsky. And I wind up sitting in his class. And unlike other times when I was in school, it's really interesting. And this guy, Ivanofsky, he can tell that I don't really like what I do. Mick, you've known that for a long time. But Ivanofsky thinks I have real insight into people. That instead of beating them, I can help them. And I like that idea. So I'm going to school and I'm going to be a psychologist.

"Getdafuck," Mickey said.

"I'm telling you. I think I got a gift for helping people with their problems."

"So you were never going to kill me?"

"Well, yeah, I was. This business here with you and these guys, I gotta clean this up for my old man before I quit."

Wanting to get things back on track, Tippy jumped in. "Excuse me. But I think we can solve all these peoples' problems if we just go with my plan. Monsieur LeMonde, if you back this show we'll work it out that you'll own a piece of Mickey's designs. And when Armand has his next designs ready, and we all believe that's going to happen, don't we?"

There was a general agreement in the room although it lacked a sense of real enthusiasm.

"Well when he has his next designs ready, Mickey can still knock them off in the states and Monsieur LeMonde can share in those profits as well. We can do that, can't we Mick?"

"Absolutely. It would be an honor to be your official knock off guy."

"So what do you think?" Tippy asked, looking to close the deal.

"And you think you can have this ready in three weeks? That's all we have," LeMonde said.

"If we can get the goods," Mickey said, his mind already in production mode. "I need something soft, semi-sheer, it should seem like it's caressing the woman."

"I know who has it." Armand said, relieved that his creative block was not going to end his life as he knew it...at least not yet...immediately he decided that helping Mickey would be easier than looking for a new job.

All eyes were on Claude LeMonde. He twirled the ends of his handlebar as he considered the offer. He pulled out a handkerchief and cleaned his monocle. He too had enjoyed the rise of Maison d'Armand both financially and being part of the glamour of the fashion world. After what seemed to be an eternity to Mickey, LeMonde approached and said, *Bon chance, Michelle Daniel. Bon chance."*

THIRTY-THREE

With only three weeks to get ready for the show and a million details to attend to, Tippy and Mickey got to work immediately. Mickey went shopping for fabrics with Armand while Tippy went to work with Armand's staff planning Mickey's first real fashion show. Nino took it upon himself to take care of another looming challenge: Charlotte. Nino suspected there was no way for Charlotte to be around if Mickey and Tippy were to reconcile. She would be a constant reminder of the troubled past. Without bothering to check with Mickey, Nino went looking for Charlotte. That turned out to be a bit more complicated than he expected. She had not turned up for work that morning so Nino went to her apartment. Nino knew her address since he had followed Mickey there while still deciding the best place to beat the crap out of him. The complication arose when Nino's knock on the door was answered by a tall Frenchman dressed only in boxer shorts.

"*Oui?*" Paul said, assuming this visitor was also French.

"I'm looking for Charlotte," Nino said while trying to look past Paul.

"And you are?"

"None of your fucking business," Nino said as he pushed his way into the apartment.

Paul went to grab Nino but Charlotte, who was still in bed, called out, "It's okay, Paul. Don't." She sat up in the bed. "What do you want, Nino?"

"Okay, listen. Mickey and Tippy are getting back together. You can't see him anymore."

"I don't want to. I told him that last night."

"Yeah, well, I don't think you can work for him anymore, either."

"Oh, really. And what the hell am I supposed to do for a job?"

"I don't know. I'll pay your way back to the States. You can find another job in the city."

"And what if I can't?"

Paul interrupted. "You can work for me. Be my bookkeeper at the garage. Don't go back."

"Don't go back? How can I not go back?" It was a thought as foreign to Charlotte as the French language.

"Stay in Paris and live with me. You know there is something special between us. I heard you say you were looking for your true love. *C'est moi, mon cher.* And you are my true love." Paul sat next to her on the bed and added, "Stay. Please."

"I don't know..."

"Hey, why not give it a shot." Nino suggested. "I'll tell you what. If you change your mind, I don't care when, I'll pay for you to come back. But you're not going back to work for Mickey. That part is out of the question."

Charlotte thought for a moment, took Paul's hand, then said, "I'll stay."

Paul leaned in and kissed her. As they held the kiss, Nino let himself out of the apartment. Mission accomplished.

Mickey and Tippy spent their day apart except for a celebratory lunch that LeMonde insisted upon. LeMonde, Armand, Tippy, Mickey, and Nino all entirely enjoyed a fabulous meal at one of Claude LeMonde's favorite restaurants. Well not everybody entirely enjoyed the meal. After a few glasses of wine, Mickey became very aware that he was seated at a table with his wife and the man who had more than likely slept with her. It was at that moment that the weight of his transgressions came crashing down. It was his infidelity that had sent Tippy to another man's bed. It was his weakness, his need to cheat and lie that had driven her crazy. He wanted to take Tippy's hand, but didn't dare. What were the new rules of engagement? When would they truly be husband and wife again? If he had his druthers things would be back to normal in an instant. But even through his wine-induced haze, Mickey knew that at some point Tippy and he would have to have "the talk." That point arrived that very night.

After work Mickey and Tippy went out to dinner. Talk was all about the new line, the show, the potential for the business, everything but what was really on their minds. Each of them took turns changing the subject to one that led them away from any discussion about the relationship. It wasn't until they were back at the apartment, when it was time for bed that "the talk" could no longer be avoided.

Mickey was already in bed, waiting for Tippy to come out of the bathroom. He lay there wondering what normal procedure was in what had turned into a very uncomfortable situation. Was he supposed to kiss her "goodnight?" Was he allowed to? Would they hug? Should they hug? It was all too complicated. When Tippy entered the room his heart began to race. Not because she looked more beautiful and alive than she had in months, although she did. It was tension that had his heart pounding in his chest.

Tippy walked to her side of the bed and took the pillow.

"I'm going to be sleeping in the other bedroom, Mick."

"Sure. Okay." He tried sounding upbeat, as if that would be just fine. But then he asked, "For how long?"

"I don't know. I guess when I trust you again." They looked at each other in silence, Tippy hugging her pillow like some kind of emotional chest protector. "I don't know if we can work things out. I'm willing to try. But, I just don't know."

"We can work things out. I know we can," he said, trying to convince himself as much as her. "When we get back to New York, do you know what we'll do?..."

"Mickey, stop. I know you want to say something that'll make things all better. But there's nothing you can say tonight that's going to change things right now. So go to sleep. Sweet dreams."

"Sweet dreams, Tip." As she headed out of the bedroom Mickey added, "You were great today."

She smiled. That didn't make things all better, but it was a start.

The next day Mickey was up early, raring to go. He slipped out to a local bakery and bought some fresh baked croissants. Next door to the bakery, a florist was just getting back from his early morning trip to the flower mart. Although not yet open for business, Mickey explained in broken Frenglish, that he desperately needed a single rose and the shopkeeper obliged. By the time Tippy shuffled into the kitchen Mickey had the coffee brewed, the table set, and the rose waiting on Tippy's plate.

"You're up early," she said.

"I'm completely jazzed, Tip. I've never wanted to go to work so much in my life."

Tippy sat down and while Mickey poured her a cup of coffee she picked up the rose and smelled it.

"This is beautiful. Thank you, Mickey."

"Yeah." There wasn't much else he could say. He was trying. He wasn't sure how many roses, or dinners, or loving looks it would take to win her back. What he was sure of was that he was determined to try.

"So what's on your agenda for today?" she asked.

"More shopping for fabric. We didn't find everything yesterday. Do you want to come too?"

The invitation touched her more than the rose. Mickey was including her. At first she hesitated. She too had been aware that the previous day's lunch was awkward, to say the least. But it wasn't as if she had any feelings for Armand. And she was pretty sure he had no real feelings for her. If she and Mickey were going to reconcile she would have to match his efforts. That was on a personal level. On a business level she loved the idea of being included. Although the line would be Mickey's creation, a woman's perspective could only help.

"I'd love to come. I'll be ready in two seconds," she said. Tippy took one last sip of coffee, got up, and took the rose. She started for the bedroom but then returned to the table. "Thanks for the rose. It's really sweet," she said before giving Mickey a tender, if all to quick, kiss before rushing off to get ready for an exciting new day.

∼

Armand had cheek kisses for both Tippy and Mickey proving that the French really are more at ease when it comes to the entanglements of the heart. Armand was completely comfortable being with both Mickey and Tippy. In fact, he found himself enjoying both their company. And even though he was still worried about his lack of inspiration, he was incredibly generous with the help he provided the aspiring designer, Michelle Daniel. That's how he introduced Mickey to each supplier they met that day. And he let them know, right upfront, that Michelle Daniel demanded only the best materials for his new line.

They bought the silkiest satins, piece-dyed taffetas so soft to the touch, the finest lace trim, they bought the richest fabrics Paris had to offer. Armand told them to spend LeMonde's money as if it were... well as if it were LeMonde's. If the line was to be as fine and elegant as Mickey imagined, they could not let price, or hell, or high water come between him and his vision. Armand explained to Mickey that he was making art and the women were his canvas.

That was all well and good. But Tippy was there to remind the artists that they should also consider price-point. One of the reasons Maison d'Armand was not a huge financial success was that his dresses were so expensive. Knock-off artists like Mickey did much more volume with Armand's designs than he could ever imagine.

It was at that moment that Tippy came up with her winning strategy. "Mickey, I think you should make things that look like they cost a million bucks but that the average woman can afford. Make beautiful things that men will want to give to their wives and girlfriends because it will be a gift for both of them. Don't make them cheap. But make them an affordable luxury. If we do that, I think we'll knock 'em dead."

"My God, you really are good at this, aren't you?" Mickey said.

"I would have sold a lot of hotdogs honey. A lot of hotdogs. But I rather be doing this."

After their shopping spree, they returned to Maison d'Armand. It was time to begin the real work. Actual patterns had to be created from Mickey's sketches. Back at T&T fashions Mickey made only four basic housecoats. The fabric might change, the trim might change, but essentially there was no design work to speak of.

Armand explained that pattern making was an art in and of itself. And usually a very time consuming art. He had some of the best people in Paris working for him. But it would be almost impossible to make patterns for the entire line in the little time they had before the show.

"You just get your people to make the patterns as quickly as possible," Mickey said. "I've got someone who can help. Someone I know can deliver what I need."

"Who do you know in Pairs?" Tippy asked.

"Not Paris. We're putting Myron Friedman on the next plane from New York."

THIRTY-FOUR

The next three weeks were a whirlwind of creation. Time had no meaning as Mickey and Tippy worked day and night. Sleeping arrangements weren't an issue since they were both exhausted by the time they got home. They each couldn't wait to get to their separate beds for what little sleep was available to them.

Mickey was right about Myron being a big help. The old cutter was rejuvenated just being back in Europe. He felt more creative than ever and was able to get Armand's designers working at New York knock-off speed. The patterns for the entire line were ready a week before the show. Fabrics had been delivered. Armand had his best seamstresses at the ready. Armand's cutter, Jean-Louis, although normally temperamental if anyone dared touch his cutting knife, was willing to step aside and let Myron Friedman cut the goods. When the first pattern was cut, Mickey and Tippy stood together watching Myron make his magic. As the electric knife made its first slice into a stack of buttery-soft silk blend, they held their breath. Tippy took Mickey's hand. He gave hers a squeeze.

Things moved along quickly. With one week to go there were still a million details to see to. Samples had to be sewn and then fitted to models. Tippy worked with Claude LeMonde on the seating chart for the show. It was critical that the important buyers had the best seats.

Then, two days before the show, Paris cab drivers went on strike. Armand feared for the worse. Buyers would have trouble getting from the airport to their hotels. They would have trouble getting from their hotels to the show. They'd have to ride on buses and subways. They'd be cranky. Cranky buyers don't buy. This was a problem they couldn't solve. Or so they thought. Once Nino heard what was going on he volunteered to go have a chat with the head of the union. He had experience dealing with unions back in New York. How different could it be in Paris?

He returned with news that it would be impossible to have cabs on the street for the buyers. Instead, they'd each have a private car with a driver at their disposal.

The day before the show was an exercise in madness. Samples were still being sewn. Nothing seemed to fit the models properly. Mickey, although calm when the day started was a complete wreck by the end of the day. Armand kept telling him that everything was alright. Calamity was the norm before every show. It always seemed like nothing was going to come together. But then, somehow, with the blessings of the gods, creation would be birthed and everything would be right with the world. Armand instructed Mickey to go home and get some rest. Armand would stay and make sure that everything was up to the standards of Maison d'Armand.

Mickey desperately wanted to believe him but the fact that he was headed home for the night before everything was finished gave him no solace.

Tippy convinced Mickey that a nice dinner might be just the thing to change his mood. It wasn't. Mickey was nervous and irritable during his dinner with Tippy and Nino. All the words of encouragement in the world would not be enough to make him relax. Once again, it was Nino, with his seemingly newfound insight into the human psyche, who had the magic words.

"Look Shithead, what's the worst that can happen?" Nino asked.

"The worst? The show is awful, nobody buys anything, we don't make any money, you decide that you have to kill me, or worse yet, I have to go back to making housecoats in which case I'll kill myself. That's the worst."

"Okay, first of all, I'm not going to kill you," Nino assured him.

"You promise?"

"I made a deal with a couple of the places where you just bought fabric. I was able to skim off enough to take care of my old man. So that's not a problem. If you want to thank someone, thank LeMonde."

Tippy raised her wine glass. "Here's to Claude LeMonde for paying those bills without saying a peep." The three clinked glasses. "And the designs are great, Mickey," Tippy said. "This is so exciting. Your first fashion show and it's in Paris. Let's enjoy it."

"I'll try," Mickey said as he downed his wine in three quick gulps. After two more glasses of wine Mickey finally calmed down. Feeling tipsy, he raised his glass, "I just want to thank you two. You're the most important people in my life. If this works out, I owe it all to you two." Mickey then put his glass down, stood up and realized he was more than just tipsy. He was quite drunk. He staggered over to Nino and gave him a big kiss on the lips. Then, while holding on to the table to steady his wobbly legs, he made it over to Tippy and kissed her, this time more tenderly than the smackeroo he gave Nino. "You two are absolutely right. It's all going to be fine," he managed to say, just before falling to floor, passed out.

Mickey awoke briefly in the middle of the night. He assumed he was either still quite drunk or dreaming because he was almost sure that Tippy was next to him in bed. He was just conscious enough to figure the vision was just part of his drunken stupor before falling back to sleep.

To his amazement, when he awoke again in the morning feeling quite hung over, Tippy still seemed to be asleep next to him. He moved his foot until it brushed her leg to make sure he wasn't still dreaming.

Tippy cracked one eye open and managed to get out a, "Wha?"

"Sorry. I didn't mean to wake you. I didn't know..." What he didn't know was what was safe to say. Was she back in the marriage bed again for good? Was it all right for him to reach out and touch her? Did she need more time? The relationship was still on very thin ice. If he brought too much attention to her being in bed with him she might not return. On the other hand she was there and he wanted to hold her. Mickey decided to apply some of Nino's advice: he would take a risk. He stretched his arm out letting it fall across Tippy's pillow. He made sure not to make contact with her yet. He felt like a thirteen-year-old boy making his first make-out move at a Saturday matinee. His heart was racing. He slowly slid his arm down the pillow until he felt her shoulder. He froze, perfectly still, waiting to see her reaction. She didn't scream. That was a good thing. But she didn't move either. He would have to risk more. Mickey edged closer so that his body was just barely touching Tippy's body. Again, she didn't move for what seemed to him to be an eternity. Then she snuggled up to him. She lay there in his arms, quietly, saying nothing. It would take a while to get things back to normal but they were moving in the right direction.

After a few minutes Tippy whispered, "Time for your big day. Let's get going." She gave him a quick kiss and popped out of bed.

Mickey watched her walk to the bathroom. She didn't know it but he felt that no matter what happened at the show, he had already had a big day.

THIRTY-FIVE

Mickey felt oddly calm amidst the chaos that was backstage before the show. Makeup artists and hair stylists were frenzied as they put the finishing touches on what seemed to be an army of beautiful women. Claude LeMonde paced nervously. The house was packed with heavyweight buyers, real success was at stake.

Tippy and Nino wished Mickey well before going out front to take their seats. They wanted to be able to see the crowd's reaction to Mickey's creations.

Mickey and Armand walked from model to model making sure each garment looked at least as fabulous as the gorgeous girl who wore it. Myron had done a great job. Armand's seamstresses had done their finest. It was show time.

Armand kissed Mickey on each cheek before wishing him, *"Bon chance, mon ami."*

"Thanks. You too," Mickey gave Armand a good old American handshake.

A glamorous crowd had gathered for the show including Janet Simpson-Parker from Bergdorf-Goodman. There was electricity in the air. For those in the fashion industry there was nothing like seeing a new line from the hottest young designers. If all went well, trends would be set. A new look might explode onto the scene. A new era might be herald in.

The house lights flashed signaling the time had come. Everyone took their seats. The excitement was palpable.

Armand walked on stage to the applause of the waiting crowd. "Thank you. Thank you all for coming. As a designer who has had many, many, many, successful shows, and has many, many, many, new ideas...

many new ideas...fabulous ideas...I do. I have decided this season to do something different. I have found an incredible new talent. And instead of showing you my many, many, many new ideas...which I can assure you I have...*Madames et monsieures,* I give you Michelle Danielle's Paris Confessions.

Lights flashed, music played, and models walked the runway in the most enticing collection of undergarments these buyers had ever seen. This wasn't the blatant trashiness from Fredrick's of Hollywood. This was something new. This collection would make every woman feel like a temptress. The show ended with a standing ovation from the audience.

Armand, with his arm around Mickey's shoulder, led Mickey down the runway. If his life depended on it, Mickey would not have been able to stop smiling. This was surreal. He was the toast of Paris' fashion elite. Armand invited the audience to stay for a reception to celebrate Mickey's first show. Over some of the best cheeses Henri had ever assembled and fine wine, buyers took turns meeting Mickey. Some insisted on having a photo taken with him.

Janet Simpson-Parker made a point of reminding Mickey, "You know technically I'm the first person to buy something from Michelle Daniel."

"Hell, you're the one who came up with the name."

"Does that mean I get a piece of the action?" she asked.

"It means you can order anything you want, as much as you want, and we'll let you pay the bills on time," Mickey, ever the salesman, said. And there was good reason for him to be selling. Armand had warned him that very often the buyers would tell a designer they loved the work but would not follow up the praise with big orders. That's what determined a successful fashion show. It wasn't the reviews of a new line in the trades or some fashion magazine. Advance orders, that's what determined success. If buyers didn't wait to see what the critics thought, or what other buyers thought, if they just went with their gut feelings and ordered goods right after the show, the designers and their financial backers would be able to sleep soundly knowing that they would be in business at least until they'd have to go through the seasonal, gut wrenching ritual again.

There was no relaxing until Claude LeMonde came out of Armand's office and reported that the line was sold out. "Based on our capacity to turn out the goods, we have sold each and every garment. Money will be rolling in and that doesn't count all the money to be made when you return to New York and Mickey begins to knock himself off."

There were congratulatory hugs and kisses all around. Armand opened a bottle of champagne. They all toasted to Mickey's newfound success and to the return of Armand's muse which, as he was assured by all, was a certainty.

For Tippy, if she was really going to run the business, there were suddenly a million details to attend to. Her mind was alive with ideas. There had been buyers at the show from all over the world. Who was going to handle production so that goods could be delivered to all the capitals of Europe? She had ideas about promotion. She knew the story of Michelle Danielle was a great story that should be told in major newspapers around the world. Who would make that happen? How long should she wait before bothering Mickey for new designs? It all could have been overwhelming. Instead it was exciting. This wasn't just Mickey's dream come true. This was her's too. Her biggest fear, living as a chemically sedated housewife being told how to live her life was no longer in the cards. She was running an international fashion house. This wasn't how she imagined her dreams being fulfilled. How could she have imagined that Mickey's infidelity, after having caused so much pain, would be the catalyst for this opportunity of a lifetime? She hoped Nino's advice was right, that with time, she and Mickey would work out their problems.

Tippy noticed that Mickey had gone back into the showroom and was sitting alone holding a glass of champagne. She left the others and sat by his side.

"You okay?" she asked.

"I don't know. We might have had a lot simpler time selling housecoats and hotdogs."

"A simpler time? Maybe. But not nearly as much fun." Tippy leaned in and kissed Mickey. Then she touched her champagne glass to his. "To exciting times...together."

They sipped champagne. He took her hand.

THE END

Made in the USA
Middletown, DE
23 October 2022